MW01620421

An isolated stretch of the North Sea coast. A place of endless tides and shifting sands. A place of blurred boundaries, where land, sea and sky merge into seamless, unknowable patterns, and where every calm surface conceals its unexpected, turbulent depths.

A man arrives to spend the overheated summer in an abandoned chalet. Adrift in his own faltering life, he slowly embraces the failed and struggling world in which he unexpectedly finds himself, existing in a kind of limbo between an unfulfilled past and an uncertain future, the days and weeks merging into a season of restless abandonment as he allows himself to be drawn into the deceptively powerful currents of the place.

Clearly drawing from the stories of both M. R. James and Algernon Blackwood, *The Wrack Line* examines the disorder, apprehension and, ultimately, the fear which forever lies beneath the calmest and most ordinary of surfaces. It is a tale of lost conviction and squandered expectation, and one in which the briefest glance of a shape in the evaporating mist or a handful of fine, warm sand trickling through trembling fingers is equal to any other horror of the world, dreamed, imagined or real.

the WRACK LINE

the WRACK LINE

ROBERT EDRIC

THE WRACK LINE

Published in September 2016 by PS Publishing Ltd. by arrangement with the author.

FIRST EDITION

ISBNs
978-1-786360-15-1
978-1-786360-16-8 [signed edition]

Design & Layout by Andrew Hook

Printed and bound in England by the T. J. International

PS Publishing Ltd
Grosvenor House
1 New Road
Hornsea, HU18 1PG
England

editor@pspublishing.co.uk
www.pspublishing.co.uk

Chapter One

I woke on that first morning to find the small room in which I had slept filled with vivid sunlight. Elsewhere over the previous months, I had become accustomed to waking at dawn or earlier—assuming I had slept at all, that is, during that unsettled and formless time—and I had become expert, as the days now brightened and lengthened, in judging the exact time of my waking; today, however, I was lost. A short, dark night had passed and, waking in that strange place, I remembered nothing of it.

It was late July, and in the city when the night was cloudless, it was light as early as four. But here—or so it seemed to me during those few uncertain minutes of my waking—it was somehow different. Also, as I say, I was waking in a place that was strange to me, and in a part of the country with which I was also unfamiliar. To add to this growing sense of disorientation, my journey there the previous day had taken considerably longer than I had anticipated or planned for. Added to which, of course, I was no longer in that city with its cacophony of far and near night-time noises—its true night and day no longer separate.

Here, the night—what little I now remembered of it—had been truly dark. The glitter of the stars above me, perhaps, a small, dim moon, the line of distant lights barely showing at the coast road's end—but, essentially, darkness.

The light now shone directly from the east, above the endless horizon of the sea, and from where I lay, on my low, makeshift bed, it was impossible to see anything outside.

I searched for my watch and saw that it was almost nine. I had slept for ten hours. I doubted if I had had a full night's unbroken sleep for the past six months. I had neither dreamed nor woken; or if I had, then both were already forgotten.

I lay without moving, feeling the warmth on my chest and arms. The sunlight fell in blocks through the two windows, its edges sharp and tangible across my skin. The thin curtains remained open, and the light lay on the narrow sills like liquid. I heard the noise of the gulls outside, their occasional landing on the roof close above me. The chalet was single storey, its roof a hollow timber frame covered with felt, and every movement of the clumsy birds was amplified. When they landed elsewhere they fell largely silent, but their continual clamour in the sky of the place meant that they were to form a constant backdrop to my time there.

I pushed myself up on to my elbows and sat with my back to the wall. There, too, the sunlight had soaked into the board and it was good to feel it against my flesh.

I looked around me. My two bags lay where I had dropped them the previous night. A few of my possessions sat on the table, and several pieces of clothing lay over the back of a chair; my shoes sat by the door. I had no memory of even this cursory unpacking.

As I say, I had arrived much later than I'd anticipated, and the taxi driver I had persuaded to bring me the final part of my journey had insisted on depositing me at the far end of the road, almost half a mile from my eventual destination. His argument for doing this was that the remainder of the path leading to the chalets was covered with blown sand and that this caused problems with his engine. He had concluded his angry speech by pointing out the lights behind us—few and intermittent though they were—and the complete darkness ahead, after which he had insisted on being paid as he had lifted my bags from his boot. When he turned and left me, I could hear his radio long after the car itself had disappeared from view.

I tried to remember if I'd made a note of his number, but guessed I hadn't. And then I tried equally unsuccessfully to remember how far I had come from the small station, where I had been the only person to alight. The taxi and its reluctant driver had been my only option.

I had imagined my destination to be only a short distance from the station, but I realised now that the journey, even in its truncated form, had lasted at least twenty minutes. There had been no meter, no measurement. The driver had told me that my train had been the last of the day, and that I'd been lucky to find him waiting there. He was scornful of my lack of foresight or preparation, and when I told him that I'd come from London, he had shaken his head and let out a long breath, as though this explained everything of me.

The station had been several miles from the village from which it took its name, and we had passed through this en route to the coast. There was a scatter of small shops, a solitary pub, and here too there were surprisingly few lights. I remember that the driver had called through his open window to a group of men standing outside the pub. He told them where he was going and that he'd soon be back to join them. Some of the men crouched down to look in at me sitting beside him. One of them said something and the remainder burst into laughter as we pulled away from them.

I was distracted from all this uncertain remembering and reckoning by a louder noise than usual above me. A bird had landed on the roof and had then scrambled to maintain its footing, screeching as it slid on the slope. Eventually, presumably, it steadied itself, returned to the ridge line and fell silent.

When I next looked at my watch, it was almost ten, meaning that I'd either been awake longer than I'd imagined, or that I'd fallen briefly back to sleep where I sat. The light and warmth that had an hour ago been across my face and chest now lay over my legs and feet, marking the progress of the rising sun in that small and brightening room.

Chapter Two

I went outside soon afterwards, intending to familiarise myself with the place at which I had arrived. I'd already had some idea of what to expect of the chalet, but I would be lying if I said that I had not expected more of the place—both of the building itself and of its desolate surroundings.

It had been described to me as a holiday home, but looking at it now, it was clear to me that the place was little used. It seemed equally unlikely to me that it had been even intermittently occupied since the previous summer. My main concern, however, was the obvious isolation of the place. I had known it was on the coast, but had anticipated—hoped—that it might at least be on the outskirts of some small town or village. But as far as I could see—and from what I remembered of the previous evening—I was at least three miles from the closest settlement.

I walked to the sandy path and looked out over the calm sea. A low concrete wall separated me from the slope of the stony beach. The worn and rounded posts of old groynes ran from the wall to the water's edge. There were numerous gaps in the timber walls where planks had been broken, washed away and never replaced.

Further along the path were a dozen or so other chalets, but from where I stood it was difficult to tell if any of these were presently occupied.

It occurred to me that without the concrete wall, both the path and the flimsy buildings themselves would have long since been lost to the ravages of the encroaching sea. Beyond the wall, the sand lay piled almost to its rim, and tall grey grass grew in clumps, binding the beach there into low dunes.

As I searched these empty surroundings, shielding my eyes from the sun, I saw a figure emerge from one of the more distant buildings—two or three hundred yards from me—cross the near-invisible path and then stand at the wall's end, looking out over the beach and sea, just as I was doing. I watched, and this distant figure did little except stand and look out over the water, occasionally moving back and forth a few paces. Then—and before I could even determine for certain whether this was a man or a woman—the figure returned to the chalet and was lost to my sight. Only then did I wish that I had either waved or called out to whoever it had been to signal my own presence in that otherwise empty place.

I was still conscious of knowing almost nothing of my surroundings, especially after the city, where everything was signposted and mapped and displayed to me every few paces, and with whose landmarks, streets and transport systems I was anyway already long familiar. Here I had only the beach and the sea stretching away on either side of me, the road and the buildings beside me, and the expanse of low and level land at my back. Even this inland horizon offered me nothing through the haze of sunlight which lay there. The opposite horizon—that of the sea—was also lost to me in its great distance, a gentle curve where the divide between water and sky was nowhere clear or definite.

I went to the low wall and climbed it, gaining a few feet perhaps, but still no true vantage point. I tried to imagine how the place might look in winter, or on a dark day, but this was difficult beneath such a vast, bright and cloudless sky.

I waited where I stood for several minutes, hoping the distant figure might reappear, or that someone else—someone closer, perhaps—might see me on the wall and come out to me. Surely, I reasoned, the appearance of *anyone* in so empty a place would be good enough reason for some degree of contact being made, however cursory or brief.

My only discovery from where I now stood was to determine that the coast road itself, having already become this sandy track, ended completely at the distant chalets. The wall, too, was gradually lost beneath the sand and grass there, buried beneath the rising dunes which continued beyond the buildings in that direction.

Seeing no one, I climbed down. The birds, which had earlier made so much noise, now floated silently in their hundreds on the sea's unbroken surface, rising and falling in the gentle swell. It was beyond me to tell whether the tide was rising or falling, or if it was so calm because it had reached that brief point of stasis precisely because it was neither approaching nor retreating. I saw the dark lines of other, higher levels along the beach above it.

Returning to the chalet, I sat at the table by the window and made a list of what I needed. Knowing now that I would have to carry everything I bought, I cut this list to its essentials. I found a rucksack in the kitchen cupboard—an ancient contraption of canvas, leather straps and buckles, and far removed from the lightweight, colourful contraptions people carried today. I shook the sand and grit from it and turned it inside out. It felt damp and smelled stale, and I laid it in the sun to dry out.

A solitary tap rose on a pipe beside the sink, and when I turned this I was hardly surprised to see nothing appear from it. The man who owned the place had told me that there was a standpipe fifty yards along the road, and that while the primitive plumbing to the individual chalets often failed, this communal water source was usually reliable. I went outside and saw the pipe attached to a timber upright at the point where the darker surface of the road disappeared beneath the sand.

Next I went out of the chalet's rear door, which jammed firmly in its frame until I threw my weight against it, and saw the lean-to with a corrugated iron roof in which—or so I had also been informed—a supply of kindling, firewood and paraffin was stored. I had imagined the place might possess a simple cooker or hotplate fuelled by a canister of gas, but I found none of these things; instead, I discovered no fewer than three small cast-iron stoves, each with its blackened, rusted grille and body.

The wood stacked against the wall of the lean-to was supplemented by a second mound piled loosely against the chalet itself. I guessed that most of this had been gathered as flotsam from the beach, and it ranged in size from clean white branches thinner than my arm to solid balks of timber salvaged from the damaged groynes. In addition to this fuel, there were half a dozen plastic sacks of charcoal. In a tin inside one of the stoves I found a box of matches.

Hanging from a solitary thin beam was a succession of lanterns, most of them still containing paraffin.

Returning indoors, I picked up the rucksack and adjusted its straps to fit my back and shoulders. It was the first time I had ever carried anything like it, and simply feeling it against my shoulders blades, hanging light and loose against my spine, gave me a simple, unaccustomed and satisfying sense of purpose.

I went back to the wall and searched for the figure I had seen earlier, but saw no one. The tide, I noticed, had started to flow more noticeably during the short time I had been inside, and a succession of gentle but distinctive waves now broke against the beach. The birds, which I had earlier counted in their hundreds, were nowhere to be seen—neither drifting on the water nor on the beach nor in the empty sky above me.

Clasping the broad and cushioned straps which hung on either side of my chest, I set off towards the road's end and the village to which this led, but which remained invisible to me beyond the inland horizon. I talked to myself as I walked, asking and then answering my own questions, and adding to my list of necessities as I went.

I reached the standpipe and tested it. Clean, cold water splashed my feet and created a stain in the sand there. I cupped my palms and drank several mouthfuls. I rinsed my face and brushed the water back through my hair, flinching at its coldness as it struck my skin.

Chapter Three

The walk to the village took me over an hour. I remembered being told by my father that, walking on the flat—and I had seldom encountered a flatter landscape—at a comfortable pace, a man might easily walk a mile in twenty minutes without the need to rest. So: three miles. I was undecided as to whether or not this was more or less than I had imagined from my sole nocturnal journey from the place.

I went to the centre of the few buildings and saw that several of the shops were closed. Upon looking closer, I discovered that most of these were in fact empty, only revealing their deserted interiors when I went closer to their dirty windows and peered inside.

I found a small convenience store that was open and went inside. Two girls waited at the till, continuing with whatever they were doing on their phones as I approached them.

'It's self-service,' one of them said to me, pointing to the pile of wire baskets I had passed. She watched me as I retraced my steps. The phone in her hand then started to trill and she turned back to it.

I started to gather together what I needed.

'You new here?' the same girl asked me. She was the older of the two, perhaps fifteen or sixteen, and she was clearly in charge of the shop.

The younger girl continued watching and jabbing at her phone. I saw that she had a carrier bag wedged between her feet, and as I came back closer to them, I saw the bag move—a sudden flex and ripple—and then fall still again. The girl saw me looking at this and kicked the bag.

'It's fish,' the older one said to me. 'Her dad fishes. Here. Off the beach. You can see the boats from over the green.' It seemed too much of an explanation, and she was keen for me to accept everything she'd said.

'I see,' I said. I left them and resumed my shopping. Neither of them spoke now, but I could feel their eyes on me as I moved up and down the few aisles of the small store.

After several minutes I returned to the counter, conscious that even the few items I had gathered might be too bulky for my bag.

'I asked if you were new here,' the girl said again as I waited for her to empty my basket.

'Holiday,' I told her.

'Holiday?' She almost laughed at the word. 'Seriously? Here?'

The younger girl walked a few paces from us and then returned. 'I can show you, if you like,' she said.

'Show me?'

She held up the carrier bag to reveal the fish inside. 'See?'

I wondered if this was a sales pitch.

'Still alive,' she said.

'I can see that.'

The other girl was clearly unhappy at this intervention and told her companion to stop bothering me.

'I was only—' the younger girl said, but knew better than to continue.

'Her father lays out nets. He's got no licence. Some have, but not him.'

'Shut up,' the younger girl said, angry and confused by this apparent sudden shift in allegiances.

'Where are you staying, then?' the girl at the till asked me. 'I'm Mary, by the way. Mary Owen. It's my mother's shop. She's Susan.'

I introduced myself to them and told them where I was staying for the next few weeks. The chalet had no name or number, and so I described its location in relation to the end of the road.

'What are you staying all the way out there for?' Susan said.

'It's owned by someone I know. A friend.'

'Owned?' Mary said. 'I thought they were all just empty and abandoned and ready to fall down. I didn't even know you *could* still live out there.'

'Apparently,' I said. 'All mod cons—walls, windows, nearby running water, the lot.' I had hoped the remark might ease the tension between us.

'What's "cons"?' Susan said.

Ignoring her, Mary said, 'The council wanted to knock the lot of them down ten years ago. When the holiday camp was supposed to be coming. There were going to be thousands of people each year. This place was going to be a goldmine.'

It sounded like a familiar story. They were hard, disappointing times.

'What happened?' I said, hardly needing to be told.

'Nothing happened. That's the whole point. The company planning the camp pulled out. They laid some of the foundations—clubhouse, indoor pool, roads—and then they decided against it and cut their losses. They even laid out the boundaries and started to fence it, but then everything stopped and all the men on the site disappeared. We had it good here for a few months and then everything vanished. Just like that. One minute, everything; the next, nothing.'

I had passed a length of high mesh fencing where the road turned inland from the sea. I had seen the cracked and overgrown foundations of the buildings in the empty fields. In the distance, I had seen the low, pale outline of a solitary structure and wondered at its purpose. The mesh fencing had ended as abruptly and as pointlessly as it had started.

'I saw it,' I said.

'Another few months and all the chalets and carriages would have been flattened and burned.'

'"Carriages"?' I said.

'Railway carriages. That's what some of them are. People bought them when the line was cut to a few trains a day and turned them into holiday homes. Most of it was done without planning permission, but the council let them stay.'

'Until the plans for the camp?' I said.

'A lot of people had already left by then. It's a hard place to live, especially in winter.'

'I can imagine,' I said.

'There was once talk of laying on electricity to the place, but nothing ever came of it. Most of the places lost their roofs and then collapsed after only a couple of winters left empty.'

'Well, there's at least one other inhabitant—visitor, whatever—out there with me,' I said, hoping to counter this litany of loss and misfortune.

'I doubt it,' Mary Owen said.

'I saw them,' I told her. 'Earlier.'

Hearing me say this, Susan Abbot looked hard at her friend, her face filled with undisguised anxiety. Perhaps they both knew exactly who else was living out at the chalets, and perhaps whoever it was, was there illegally.

'I'm sure I'll meet whoever it is,' I said.

'I suppose so,' Mary said, adding, 'She'll still sell you the fish, if you want them.'

'What are they?' I asked the younger girl, happy to change the subject.

'Two whiting, one bass,' she said. 'Can't you tell?' She again held up the bag for me to look inside. At least one of the fish was still alive and writhing slightly.

I offered the girl ten pounds and she accepted it.

'You paid over the odds,' Mary said, smiling to herself and shaking her head.

I was going to say something about what I might normally have paid for the fish, but thought better of this and stayed silent. I packed what little I had bought into the rucksack.

'That all you got?' Mary asked me. She searched behind the counter and produced two more carriers. 'Which way did you come?' she said, repacking what I'd bought.

The pair of them laughed when I told them I'd followed the coast road and then turned inland at the abandoned camp.

'He followed the road,' Susan repeated. 'All the way from that dump.'

'To this one,' Mary added.

'You sound as though you're getting ready to abandon the place yourselves,' I said.

'Like a shot. When the opportunity arrives,' Mary said. 'While I've still got the chance.' It was a vapour of fading hope, and I knew even as she said it that she too understood that. 'There's a path,' she said. 'Directly from here to the end of the road and close behind the chalets. Nobody will stop you. It's half the distance. Look over there.' She pointed to the shop window behind me and I turned to look. 'Between the church and the house next to it.'

A narrow alleyway disappeared quickly into shadow.

'Follow that lane and you'll see the path ahead of you. There are plank bridges over most of the dykes. You won't see them until you get to them, but they're there.'

I tested the weight of my bags and told her I was grateful for her help.

'That's me,' she said. 'Helpful.'

I smiled at the remark and she smiled back at me.

When I left, she walked outside with me, telling the younger girl to remain in the empty shop.

Outside, she said, 'Were you serious about other people living out there?'

'I definitely saw somebody,' I said. 'Or perhaps it was someone from here just walking on the beach.'

She considered this. 'Not that far out,' she said. She looked around us as she spoke. 'When they were still going ahead with the camp, one of the things they were going to do was to raise and extend the sea wall so the place would be properly protected. It floods, see. It's why most people finally left. Either that or the sand blows into everything. Not what paying holidaymakers want for their money, is it?'

'No, I suppose not,' I said, still uncertain why she remained so insistent on these explanations.

She crossed the small green with me to the entrance of the lane. Fifty yards ahead of me, back out in the bright sunlight, I saw the path leading back towards the sea. I could see neither the coast road nor the chalets from where I stood, but I knew I was at least looking in the right direction.

'What will you do?' Mary asked me unexpectedly as we parted.

'Do?'

'I mean, out there. You might *say* you're on holiday, but it's not that kind of place. It might have been, once, but not now.'

'I'm not really certain,' I admitted to her. 'Rest, I suppose. Recuperate.'

'From what?'

'Sorry?'

'You said "recuperate".' She hesitated at my reaction to this.

'I meant rest,' I said. 'Just rest. I've had a lot on recently. I'm mostly here just to get away from everything. From the world at large, I suppose. The Madding Crowd and all that.'

She smiled at the remark. 'Well, you've certainly come to the right place for that,' she said.

Across the road, Susan called out that someone was waiting to be served. I hadn't seen anyone else enter the shop in the few minutes we'd been standing together.

I thanked Mary again for her directions and set off along the narrow alleyway. It was much cooler in the permanent shadow of the adjoining building and I felt this on every inch of my exposed skin. I quickened my pace and soon came back out into the light and warmth beyond. The more distant surroundings were again lost to me in the glare of the sun, but I was at least able to follow the path of trodden grass and baked earth as it now revealed itself ahead of me.

After only fifteen minutes of walking, I was able to make out the sea and the pale line of the road, and beyond this the vague shapes of the scattered dwellings at its end.

CHAPTER FOUR

Later that evening, having finally eaten for the first time since my arrival, and having rearranged the chalet's few pieces of furniture—more specifically, having turned my bed so that I would not wake at the first early light of the dawn—I left the place and crossed the road to the beach.

I climbed on to the sea wall and waited there, again hoping to attract the attention of whoever else might be there. Everything the two girls had revealed to me had that there was no one else currently staying here.

After twenty minutes of having seen no one, I climbed down from the wall and walked along the beach in the direction of the abandoned camp, soon finding myself beyond all sight of the chalets.

The coast curved, but only gently, and so the view both ahead of me and behind me changed only slowly. Distant landmarks—vague though these remained—came and went in both directions before I had even noticed them. It was difficult for me to gauge how far I had walked. In places the beach was firm—more pebble than sand—and elsewhere the sand was loose and soft and difficult to walk on, and I felt the ache in my calves and thighs after only a few paces. To my right, the distant low curve of the sea remained the same wherever I went.

I stopped after an hour, rested for a few minutes on a balk of timber, and then turned back and retraced the line of my footsteps.

The day's light was fading by then, and I expected to see the lights of the village and its roads ahead of me, but instead there was only the inland darkness. There was not a single light ahead of me, and only by diverting from my course and walking close to the water's edge did I finally see a cluster of dim lights in the distance. The sand closer to the retreating tide was compacted and firm and so I was able to move more swiftly towards my goal.

I was relieved when, after only a few more minutes of walking, I was finally able to make out the line of lights along the coast road. I daresay I had been immersed in complete darkness for only a few minutes—five at the most, perhaps—and yet the effect this had had upon me was undeniable. I could feel my heart beating—although I daresay this was as much a result of the soft sand further up the beach as anything else.

Continuing back, I finally came to a part of the beach I recognised, and I stopped to rest. Somewhere in the distance, a car was started and then driven noisily into the darkness. I could hear it moving away from me for several minutes in the surrounding silence.

To the west, the sun, although already lost beneath the distant horizon, made clear the distinction between the land and the sky. But to the east, above the line of the sea, this divide was again lost, and the darkness of the water merged imperceptibly with the darkness of the sky above it. Higher still, the brighter constellations were clearly visible to me.

I walked until the low outlines of the chalets themselves were revealed to me against the dying light.

When the wall began, I climbed back up onto it and walked along its broad surface. I saw by my watch that I had been out for over two hours. It was longer than I had imagined, though perhaps the unchanging perspective and the fading light had had something to do with this. My only intention now was to return to the chalet, pour myself a drink, read, perhaps—if I could coax one of the lanterns into working—and then go to my bed. In addition to my legs, my back and shoulders now ached.

And it was then, as I was about to climb down from the wall and cross the road, that I saw ahead of me the same figure I had seen earlier. Or at least I assumed it was the same person—they looked similar in outline and stood at roughly the same place as at my previous sighting. I waited where I stood, wondering whether or not I could be seen by whoever it was. There was every likelihood that I would be totally invisible in the darkness which now surrounded me, and the last thing I wanted was to alarm them by appearing so unexpectedly like this, and so close to them. I calculated that the distance between us was a hundred yards. And so I remained silent. I watched the figure closely and saw that—as earlier—whoever it was gave no indication of having seen me. And as I watched, the figure moved from the road to the wall and then on to the beach; a short, effortless journey towards the water.

And as it moved, I knew finally that the figure was a woman.

The wall upon which I stood four or five feet above the sand appeared to present no obstacle to her, and I realised that this was because it was mostly buried in that direction, with a gentle slope of sand rising to its rim on both sides. One of the reasons I was convinced it was a woman was because she held her arms folded at her chest, and because her pace was even and slow. She rose and then she fell, and not once did she break her stride.

Moving a few yards on to the beach, she paused and looked around her, and I instinctively crouched where I stood, still conscious of how alarming I might appear to someone not expecting to see anyone in that otherwise empty place.

I need not have worried: she looked towards me and then beyond me, and then she continued turning her head until she was facing in the opposite direction completely. Nothing distracted her and nothing gave her reason to pause.

It was beyond me now to do anything to reveal myself to her, and so I dropped quietly from the wall and stood on the opposite side to her. I was still able to see her where she stood on the beach, but I was confident that however hard she looked towards me I would remain invisible to her.

I felt uncomfortable, watching her like this—knowing perhaps that she too imagined herself to be completely alone in the place—and so I made my way as quietly as possible back to the chalet. Only when I reached my door did I turn and look back to where she stood with her back to me, continuing to stare out over the sea. The water's edge came close to her feet, and the gently breaking waves were faintly luminescent in the moonlight.

I thought then, as I was about to go indoors, that I heard her voice, that she was saying something, singing perhaps, or simply humming a tune. But as swiftly as I formed this impression, so it was gone. Perhaps all I had heard had been the call of roosting birds, or the noise of the water on the shore; perhaps even only the night breeze playing across the grass and dunes or the inland fields.

I waited, straining to hear more, but nothing came.

And then she turned and came back up the beach to the wall, passed over this to the road, and continued walking until she was lost to sight amid the distant chalets.

I waited where I stood, hoping to see a light appear at the window of one of the buildings, but after ten minutes there was still nothing. It was too dark, and I was still too far away from her to see which of the chalets she might have entered.

I waited a short while longer, and then went inside, where, having no success with any of the lanterns, I lit several candles and poured myself a drink. I felt suddenly very tired—guessing this to be the combined effect of the sea air and all the walking I had done that day—and soon afterwards I fell asleep.

CHAPTER FIVE

The following morning, feeling well rested after a second undisturbed night, I decided to visit the distant chalets, to seek out and finally introduce myself to whoever was staying there. It seemed ridiculous to be sharing so isolated a place with someone else and to remain unknown to them. Regardless of how the woman responded to this, we would at least then be aware of the other's presence and afterwards make all the necessary allowances.

I left the chalet late and followed the track alongside the wall. The sand in this direction had encroached much further inland, and the few dwellings I passed had long since become derelict and uninhabitable. The sand had blown, shifted and gathered around them, burying their small gardens and mounding against their walls. Where the glassless windows had not been boarded up, I looked inside and saw the sand there too, level across the floors and piled in smooth screes where the wind had blown inside. Some of the flimsy buildings had clearly been empty for years—decades, perhaps—and yet something about the appearance of some of the shacks and converted carriages caused me to think that they had only recently been abandoned to the elements, and that someone had once cared enough for them to protect them and live in them until their inevitable loss was no longer avoidable.

Some of the empty rooms still had furniture scattered around them; tattered curtains and blinds still hung at some of the windows. In one chalet, a chair and sofa and table still stood where they had finally been abandoned. I even saw a bookcase filled with sodden, dirty books standing where it had been left. Perhaps someone had gone away from the place fully intending to return, but had then, for one reason or another, never come back. Perhaps distant owners had died and no one else had wanted the places enough to even come and look at them. Or perhaps, after years of persistence and struggle—against those elements and the distant, uncaring machinery of bureaucracy—that struggle had become too great, too time-consuming or too costly—and the dwellings and their few worthless contents had finally been abandoned to their fate without a backward glance or second thought or moment of regret.

As I examined these empty shells I kept a watch for the woman, who, seeing me approach so close to where she lived, would surely come out to me—even if it was only to tell me that she didn't appreciate my intrusion into her own isolation there.

There were further abandoned buildings beyond the path's end, and these were the most dilapidated of all—every one of them without its roof and few with their doors or windows intact.

I went to where I believed I had seen the woman and looked among the few buildings there for where she might live. But none of the structures looked to be even remotely inhabitable, let alone actually lived-in. Everything there was in a state of complete ruin and abandonment. Perhaps I had come too far from the path's end. But even as I considered this, I knew that behind me too I had passed nothing that suggested anyone had recently been living there. Or perhaps there were homes further inland, beyond the dunes and the field boundaries. Perhaps I had seen someone at the beach who had merely passed *through* the cluster of empty chalets on their way to the water's edge. I had certainly not seen the woman actually enter any of the buildings, and on both occasions I had only ever watched her from a distance, and on my last sighting in darkness.

I came eventually to the last of the structures—little more than two walls of grey plasterboard, supported now by the dune which had built up inside them. Charred timbers and scattered litter were the only other signs that anyone else had been there in the recent past.

Turning away from the sea, I followed a track through the hummocky land towards the first of the fields. The land here was covered in brambles and sharp grass. The path I followed looked well-trodden, suggesting that it was in regular use.

I came to a dyke and walked to the concrete slab of a bridge which spanned it. I sat on the bank there and searched around me. I could make out the distant village and the line of a path leading towards it. In all likelihood, it then occurred to me, this was where the woman had gone. I was surprisingly disappointed by this realisation: I truly was alone where I was staying; I had no company.

I waited where I sat for several minutes, deciding what to do with the rest of the day ahead. I had sufficient provisions for the immediate future, but I would soon have to return to the village and the shop to build up a proper supply.

When I finally rose and began my return journey, I saw someone coming towards me along the path. The figure raised a hand to me and waved. I knew immediately that it wasn't the woman. I raised my own hand in response and waited where I stood. The water in the dyke flowed slowly beneath me.

Several minutes later, the man, having diverted from his course to cross the invisible drains and come to me, reached me at the bridge.

He held out his hand to me. 'Alex Lister,' he said. He nodded over his shoulder. 'I live in the village. And you're our mysterious visitor.'

'I'm hardly that,' I said. I introduced myself to him and tried to point to where I was staying, but the chalets could not be seen from where we stood. I was surprised by this, guessing that the dunes and overgrown land through which I'd come had been higher and more extensive than I'd thought.

'Oh, I know everything about you and where you're staying. It's that kind of place. Were you on your way to the village?'

'Just walking,' I said. 'Hoping I might run into whoever else was staying out here.' I waited for his response to this.

He pursed his lips and shook his head. 'I doubt there's anyone else,' he said. 'A few years ago there'd be the odd visitor, the occasional family come to pick over the ruins. A decade back, there were approaching fifty habitable chalets out here. And now I doubt if even a handful could be used. Besides, if the County Council finally gets its way, you might even be our last ever visitor.'

'Oh?'

'They've been slapping Unfit Dwelling Orders on every place left empty for the past three years. First they wanted the land—'

'For the holiday camp.'

'Which never materialised. And then just to get the land cleared and ready for whatever might come next.'

'Such as?' I said. It seemed unlikely to me that the inaccessible and unstable land could ever become anything other than what it already was.

'Exactly,' he said. 'Although at one time there was talk of building a visitor centre, and then a lodge park—not on the beach as such, but back here.' He swung his arm across the nearby fields. 'That's the thing about this place—there's always something *about* to happen, always something just around the corner.' He took out a packet of cigarettes and offered me one. I hesitated for a moment and then accepted. Who was there close enough to me now to tell me what harm I might be doing to myself?

'I thought I'd stopped,' I told him, crouching to his lighter and cupping my hands around it.

'I suffer from the same delusion,' he said.

I sucked the smoke into my lungs and then let it out in a long, slow breath.

'Mary Owen told me all about you,' he said. 'Just in case you were wondering.'

'The girl in the shop?'

'And the fount of all local knowledge,' he said.

'Every tiny scrap of which is endlessly embroidered and speculated upon?'

'Something like that. Like I said, it's a small place.'

'So what *will* eventually happen to the chalets?' I asked him.

He shrugged. 'I daresay it hardly matters. You've seen the place. Would *you* gamble on their future?'

There was no answer to this.

He went on: 'When the holiday camp failed, it somehow set the pattern for everything that's happened since.' He looked towards the sea, and then hesitated slightly before adding, 'What made you think there was someone else out here besides yourself?' His gaze remained fixed on the horizon as he waited for my answer.

'I saw someone,' I said. 'Last night, and earlier in the day. It looked like the same person, a woman.'

'People come and go all the time,' he said. 'Especially in the summer. Visitors, walkers, the occasional angler when the tide's right.'

'She's the only person I've seen,' I said.

'The village kids come and light fires out here. It's where the older ones sometimes come to drink and . . . well. Ask Mary Owen the next time you're in the shop. On warm nights, they sometimes even sleep out here.'

I remembered the charred timbers and scattered litter.

'All Not Allowed, of course,' he said smiling.

'Which is precisely why they do it?'

'Half the fun, I suppose. Besides, there's not a great deal else locally to keep them entertained.' He pointed in the direction of the failed camp and then out over the sea. 'There used to be a line of villages out there. All under the water now, of course. The last of them lost only two hundred years ago.'

'"Only"?'

He laughed. 'Believe me—it's nothing where this part of the world's concerned.'

'A church spire seen only at the lowest tide? A ghostly bell still tolling for lost souls?'

He smiled at this. 'Sadly, not even that. Before I retired, I worked in the Museum and Archive Service. It's all very well documented.'

'Have you always lived here?' I asked him.

'Forty years. My wife died. Recently. Cancer. I took care of her. We were told she had much longer.'

'I'm sorry,' I said.

'It left me high and dry,' he said, shaking his head. 'We'd always intended going somewhere more . . . convenient.'

'Somewhere less isolated?'

'I suppose so. Not that I mind the isolation. Besides . . . ' He closed his eyes and held his face to the sun. 'Besides, if you feel the isolation now, you should come back in the winter.'

'I can imagine,' I said.

'It's the best way—imagining, I mean, not experiencing.'

I told him I'd take his word for that.

Then he looked at his watch and said it was time for him to return. 'Come and see me,' he said. 'In fact, come for dinner. Not tonight. Wednesday, three days.'

I accepted the offer and he told me his address, describing his home in relation to the shop I had already visited.

He left me after that and retraced his path back through the fields. I had hoped he might stay longer, and I felt my second vague and unaccountable stab of disappointment that morning. Unlike my fleeting glimpses of the woman—who I now accepted was unlikely to be actually staying in any of the decrepit chalets—I was able to watch Alex Lister continuously until he was finally lost to sight behind a hedge halfway back to the village.

I returned to the centre of the dunes, climbing until I was again able to see the coast road and the buildings along it. I waited and searched for several minutes, my eyes shielded against the sun, but apart from the barely-moving swell of the sea and the rise and fall of a small flock of birds, there was no other movement. Sweat ran from my brow into my eyes, and from my cheeks to the corners of my mouth.

Chapter Six

Over the next few days it grew even warmer. The sky remained cloudless and the air stayed calm. Beneath its thin roof, the chalet became airless and overheated, its doors and windows permanently open, even through the night. But despite all this, I still managed to sleep, and I continued to wake each morning refreshed, and even anticipating with pleasure the empty day ahead.

I filled every container I could find and built up a supply of water. I wandered around in shorts and sandals. I spent whole mornings and afternoons just walking and reading. I dismantled and cleaned the lanterns and finally got them to work. It was a simple enough thing, and yet it seemed a great achievement to me.

During the following days, I saw nothing of the woman at the end of the path. I kept an intermittent watch in that direction, but she never reappeared. I wondered if my own arrival there had anything to do with this, but even as this occurred to me, I knew it was unlikely.

I walked frequently on the beach, and I explored further the paths and lanes which latticed the fields and open land. I found out where all the simple bridges had been laid, and which drains appeared to be always full and running, and which were lined with dried, cracked mud. Individual cows and small groups of cattle stood and watched me as I made all these casual explorations.

Occasionally, figures would appear on the beach or further along the surfaced road, but few of these either left the water's edge or diverted their course to the ruined chalets. I discovered that a long-distance coastal path ran along the line of the sand-blown road, but that this was little used, and that most of its followers preferred to walk on the beach. This suited me. The low wall hid the chalet from most walkers, and those few who did come closer to it were content to either carry on walking and ignore me completely, or to acknowledge me with no more than a raised hand or a nod. Some were surprised by my presence there; others, I imagine, probably believed I was there illegally, squatting perhaps, or a dispossessed former owner claiming the last of his dying rights.

On one occasion, a woman asked me what I thought I was doing there—her tone clear to me—and I told her boldly it was where I lived. "I don't *think* so," she said to me, and then turned and continued walking. Her husband signalled his apology to me with a tired glance. I was sitting outside on my rattan chair, a book in my lap, a drink beside me. I saw the envy in his eyes and I raised my drink to him as they went.

Three days after I'd met him, I went to see Alex Lister, calling first at the village shop. I gave the woman now at the counter there the list I had made. I hoped she could somehow deliver the groceries to me, or that I could again engage the reluctant taxi driver.

I chose two bottles of wine from her small selection and she wiped these with a cloth before handing them to me.

I was about to leave the shop when Mary Owen called from the back room and then came out to us.

'Thought I recognised the voice,' she said. She was wearing a short skirt, and a top which revealed her stomach. She was barefoot and her hair was wet. She brushed this as she came in to us. 'Remember me?' she said.

'Of course.'

'Thought you'd be back sooner than this. What are you living on out there?'

'I manage,' I said. 'Besides . . . ' I indicated the woman, who I assumed to be her mother, and who was now gathering my items from the shelves. 'I'm stocking up.'

The girl watched her mother for a moment and then came closer to me, indicating the door. I went outside with her.

'I didn't want her hearing,' she said, adding to the sudden mystery and drama of her appearance.

'About what?' I guessed she was going to confess about being at the chalets and whatever happened there.

She considered me closely for a moment, squeezing the last of the dripping water from her hair, and then pushing it back over her bare shoulders. I felt its fine spray on my face.

'You saw her,' she said.

'Saw who?'

'Old man Lister was in earlier, asking if any of us—me, he meant—had been out that way, messing about in the empty chalets. You don't need to be a genius to work out what he was really saying.'

'I met him a few days ago,' I said. 'In fact, I'm on my way to see him now.'

'I can see that. Nobody buys wine here. What did he tell you?'

'That all sorts of people wander out there and that—'

She gave a forced laugh. '"All sorts of people"? What, in the middle of the night? People who appear and then just vanish?'

I wondered at the force of these uncertain denials, at what she believed Lister might have told me.

'Look,' I said, 'I saw someone—that's all. At first, I imagined it might be someone staying on one of the other chalets. I made a guess and I got it wrong. No real mystery.'

She smiled at this. 'Which chalet was it you imagined she was living in? Further along from your dump? Nearer to the end of the path? You'll have been for a closer look by now, I suppose.'

'Perhaps.'

She shook her head. 'You should hear yourself.'

I was becoming both irritated and confused by her evasive provocations. 'So who was she, then?' I said. 'Who did I see? Was it you? One of your friends? There was certainly *someone* on the path and then later on the beach. And *someone's* had a fire in the dunes and been out there recently.'

'Nothing to do with what *you* saw,' she said. She was calm now, and smiling again. She took one of the bottles from me. 'You opening this, or what?'

I laughed at the remark.

'Suit yourself.'

I took the bottle back from her. Neither of us spoke for a moment. I watched the woman in the shop. She held my list close to her face.

'She can hardly see,' Mary Owen said. 'She's got glasses, but she never wears them. Vanity, see?'

I guessed the woman to be in her early forties, still young.

I pointed to her wet hair. 'Going out somewhere?' The wetness had soaked into her top.

'Might be. What, you think we're all off to the dunes for an orgy, or something?' She laughed again at the suggestion, making me uncomfortable, cautious.

'All I meant—'

'I know what you meant. Besides, it's miles away. Better things to do closer to home.' She raised her hand to a group of youths congregating in the pub car park.

'I can imagine,' I said.

'No you can't.' She turned away from me to watch her mother.

'So tell me the story,' I said. 'About the mysterious woman. Is she the ghostly grieving widow of a drowned sailor waiting for him to return to her? Did they once live in a house where the chalets now stand?'

My flippancy angered her. Whatever she had been about to reveal to me, I had defused and disparaged. I could see all this in the sudden sag of her face, and the instant I understood this, I regretted what I'd done.

She turned away from me and remained silent. I wondered what to say to her. But when she turned back to me she was smiling again. Her eyes were narrowed and her lips were thin, revealing nothing of her teeth. The word "sly" came into my head. Then just as swiftly as it had appeared, the smile fell from her face. She wiped a hand across her mouth and then looked at her palm.

'Well . . . ?' I said. I felt a dryness in my throat.

'Well what?'

'The woman?'

'You know it all already,' she said. 'People like you always do.'

'I'm sorry,' I said.

'What for? For knowing better than everybody else, everybody here?'

'For not listening to your explanation.'

'Who says it's an explanation? It's just a story.'

But I knew that I had guessed at enough of this particular story—at its essentials, at least, if not its precise or variable details—to still undermine what she had been about to tell me.

'Have *you* seen her?' I said.

The question caught her unawares. 'I might have.' The words were a reflex and might have meant yes or no. She was still angry that I had defused her tale.

'Do you believe in them?' she asked me.

'Ghosts?' I considered my answer. I closed my eyes for a moment. Opening them, I saw her watching me closely. 'I believe people are haunted by things,' I said. 'Things they've done, things unfinished, unresolved; things they regret.'

'But not in ghosts themselves?'

'I don't know. Perhaps they're all part of the same thing—you know, something inside a person that manifests itself in something external.' I was floundering, uncertain of what exactly I was saying to her, of what I *wanted* to say; and uncertain too whether it was what I myself truly believed, or if it was merely a convenient explanation or confession that kept all its options open.

And as though reading this tangle of confused thoughts, she smiled again and said, 'Is that a "yes" or a "no", then?'

I confessed to her that I didn't really know.

'In that case—' she began to say, and was then interrupted by a shout from one of the boys in the car park.

'You're in demand,' I said.

'Me? Always.'

'I'd still like to hear it,' I said. 'The story of the woman.'

The remark made her suspicious. 'It's an old story. Everybody here knows it. Ask old man Lister.'

'So have others seen her?'

'Some,' she said, again turning away from me and lowering her voice as she spoke.

'You included?'

'No.' This time she looked directly at me and spoke firmly.

'Oh, I thought—'

'It doesn't really matter to me what you think,' she said. Everything she said to me tipped a balance one way or another, her every remark and answer an unsettling denial of something she had seemed happy to be about to share or confirm only a moment earlier.

'No, I suppose not,' I said.

'But *you* definitely saw her, right?'

'Like I said—I saw *someone*,' I said.

She saw this for the evasion it was and shook her head. 'And like *I* said, ask Lister. He's another know-it-all.'

The boys on the wall called again, and without another word to me, she turned her back on me and crossed the road towards them.

In the shop, the woman continued packing bags. She saw me looking in at her, and then looked from me to her departing daughter. I nodded to her and she returned the gesture before disappearing from view behind a shelf.

Chapter Seven

A hallway led directly to the rear of the house. The two doors on either side of the entrance were closed, casting this high, narrow corridor into shadow.

Alex Lister walked ahead of me into the room overlooking his back garden. A table had been laid at the window there. The garden itself was long and overgrown, and beyond it lay the open land stretching to the coast.

The hallway walls were covered with nondescript landscapes and framed photographs, mostly, I suspected of Lister's dead wife; the room beyond likewise. The first thing that struck me about the house was its air of neglect and emptiness, and I felt upon going into that rear room—and despite the recently laid table there—that it had not been used for some considerable time. Everything seemed faded and stale. The furniture—of which there was too much, and all of which was old and heavy and dark—was scuffed and worn. The rug at the empty fireplace was frayed at its edges and had bald patches. Ash and pieces of unburned coal sat in the large hearth. A film of dust lay over the ornate and cluttered marble mantel.

I went first to the window and looked out, the falling sun already casting its long shadows towards the sea.

'You were talking to the Owen girl,' Lister said, coming to stand beside me.

'She was telling me in a roundabout way about your ghost,' I said, my scepticism clear to him.

He took the bottles from me and stood them on the table, where a third was already opened and waiting. He poured two glasses and gave me one. The glass was engraved crystal, and like much else in the place, over-elaborate. Everything, it seemed, shouted only of the lost past and of the life he had once lived there with his wife.

'Which story did you get?' he said, but with little enthusiasm.

'Are there variations?'

He laughed. 'Of course there are. All depending on who's telling the tale, and why.'

'And on the gullibility of the listener?'

'Naturally. So?'

'Sorry?'

'Which version?' He made the remark sound casual, but I could sense that he wanted my answer.

'She didn't tell me much,' I said. 'I pre-empted her with my own guessed tale of a waiting, grieving wife'—I regretted the word even as I said it—'and disappointed her.'

'I see. Did you meet the mother?'

'In the shop.'

'The place is bankrupting her. She keeps saying this will be the last summer there. The girl herself, of course, will be off like a shot—they all will—at the first opportunity.'

I went closer to the mantel and indicated the photograph of the woman at its centre.

'Elizabeth,' he said fondly. 'My wife. If she'd lived, we'd probably both be long gone ourselves from the place. This house was her parents' home, where she grew up. She had plans to strip it all out and completely redecorate and refurbish it. She wanted to build a conservatory and move the kitchen. She would have put in another bathroom. Big plans. Everything more manageable, easier to live in. And then she—well, you can guess the rest.'

'Her illness.'

He sipped at his wine. 'After which, I suppose a kind of inertia set in—in the place itself, in me. I retired early to take care of her, and when she died I was left here high and dry.' He gestured to the chairs in the window. 'Sorry. Please.'

We went and sat overlooking the untidy garden.

'If you like, I can show you pictures of the chalets in their heyday, when they were all still lived in and when the place was a proper community. When Elizabeth was ill and I was looking after her—I won't call it "nursing"—I started to compile a history of the village. I began to realise what had been lost here, and then to understand what was yet likely to go. It sometimes seems to me that the place has done nothing *except* struggle against its own end.'

It seemed a strange, almost prophetic remark to make, but I let it pass.

'And the chalets in particular?' I said.

'I suppose so. The coastline is forever moving and changing. Stable for a few decades, perhaps, and then altering completely over the course of a single winter.'

'Was your wife—Elizabeth—from here, then?'

'Her father owned a farm bordering the sea road. When he died, the land was divided up and sold off. It wasn't worth much; not then, not now.'

'So the family wouldn't have stood to gain by the holiday camp?'

He laughed at the suggestion. 'Far too late for that. Besides . . . '

I waited, eventually saying, 'Besides, it was never a viable prospect?'

'Something like that. Are you hungry?'

I was. Throughout my short time in the place, I seemed to be constantly hungry, and yet also to have already lost some weight. My shirts felt looser, as did my waistbands.

He left the room briefly and returned with two plates, upon each of which was a plastic container—one holding slices of cold ham, the other a simple potato salad. I had been anticipating—and hoping for—considerably more.

'I hope it's enough,' he said, putting food on each plate. 'I should have made more of an effort in your honour. Visitors are something of a rarity these days. And, as you can imagine, we're somewhat limited locally in our choice.'

The nearest supermarket was only twenty minutes away by car.

'There's bread and cheese for later. And fruit. Elizabeth was the cook. You might say I've developed a taste for the simpler things in life, food and drink included.'

We ate and talked, swapping our histories—or at least as much of them as we could each bring ourselves to reveal and share. It helped us both, I imagine, to know that the other man was a stranger, and that, beyond the following few weeks, we were unlikely ever to see each other again.

After we had eaten, and when the second of my bottles had been opened, he took a heavy album from one of the room's sideboards and brought it to the table. I saw the mound of others from which it was selected, and which he pushed back into place having made his choice.

The book was laid between us and opened. Sheets of tissue were interlaced between its mounts.

'Photos and postcards,' he said. 'The sea road. As far as I've been able to piece it together, the first of the carriages was brought here soon after the Great War.'

'As long ago as that?'

'Makeshift homes. Men claiming what they believed they had a right to claim for themselves. There were at least three dozen of the things there by the mid-Twenties, after which the place just grew. It wasn't until after the Second War that any planning regulations began to be applied, by which time there were upward of eighty structures stretching nearly two miles from the coast road proper to where the dunes are now spreading again.'

He pointed out the photographs and postcards he had found. There was even a pamphlet published to encourage people to exercise their rights as squatters and to permanently inhabit the site.

'In the last war, people evacuated their homes in the nearby towns and moved into the chalets to keep themselves safe.' He listed half a dozen places, some over thirty miles distant, from which the people had come, though none of these struck me as the likely targets of a bombing raid.

'Propaganda,' he said. 'First the authorities wanted people out of the cities, and then they tried to stop them from leaving and taking on these temporary homes for themselves. Bad for morale—all these people running away and taking the law into their own hands.'

'What happened?'

'For the duration, nothing much. Other priorities, I suppose. But afterwards, I think there was a general acceptance that everything had gone too far—a free-for-all—and that people had to start observing the rules again, about what they could and couldn't do on land over which they had no genuine claim.'

'So were people actually evicted from the place?' I turned the pages as I spoke, searching for a photograph of my own temporary home.

He saw me doing this. 'Next page,' he said, smiling.

I turned the page and saw a photograph of the chalet in its prime.

'That's yours,' he said. 'The picture was taken in 1947. I imagine the thing was only a few years old, five at the most.'

The chalet was surrounded by a fence enclosing a small garden. A path ran from a low gate to the door, which had a trelliswork porch attached to it. All these features had long since disappeared, along with any vestige of the garden itself.

'Is this the only picture?' I asked him.

'I'm afraid so. Somebody's pride and joy.'

'It would have been intriguing to have seen someone standing in the doorway,' I said.

'Or perhaps a shadowy face at one of the windows?'

'I suppose so.'

'Turn the page,' he said.

I did this.

'Bottom right-hand.'

I looked more closely at the photograph. It showed a path and several of the buildings—no solitary feature—and a scatter of people standing around the structures.

'Where is it?' I asked him.

'It's the road's end. The wall hasn't been built yet and the sand hasn't encroached and buried the road.'

'So these are all now abandoned and lost.'

He nodded. 'It took me a while to work it out, but two of the buildings—the two at right angles to each other—had brick chimneys built up their outside walls.' He pointed to the structures. 'The chimneys toppled long ago, but their bases are still there. Mostly buried. I can take you to the end of the wall and show you exactly where the shot was taken.'

'Do you know when?'

'Someone's written 1951 on the back. It would probably fit. At least thirty of the buildings were still permanently inhabited ten years after that, when the local council first started to get serious about controlled development and evictions. I count fourteen people looking at the photographer.'

I looked again at the small crowd.

Reaching behind him, Lister took a magnifying glass from a drawer and handed it to me.

'What am I looking for?'

'This was the photograph used in the local paper when the tale of there being a ghostly woman wandering the site started doing the rounds. The editor asked for readers to write and tell him of their own sightings and encounters—'

'And, surprise surprise, they came flooding in?' I searched the magnified figures. Any one of a dozen of them could have been the woman I had seen almost a week earlier.

'And with each of the so-called sightings a small and spurious history or vague recollection of something once having happened at the place was attached,' he said. 'I made a study—if that's the word—of every one that was printed.'

'Were any of them ever remotely credible?'

'One or two. Not "credible" necessarily, but with some basis in truth. Not that any of these "truths"—facts, say—were proof of subsequent ghostly appearances or hauntings. People lived and died out there, just as they did everywhere else.'

'But nothing which stood out?'

He took the magnifying glass from me and studied the picture himself. 'All this used to make Elizabeth angry. Why go looking for so-called ghosts, she said, when the world was already filled with the terrors and uncertainties of the living and the dying. And that was before she was diagnosed. You can imagine her feelings on the subject afterwards. To be honest, until the Owen girl told me about you being out there and what you imagined you'd seen, I hadn't given the stories much thought for years. Like everywhere else'—he looked at the room around us, already darkening as the sun retreated from it—'I let things drift, slip, float beyond my interest and concern.' He closed the album. 'Everything, one way or another, unravels to its unhappy, unexpected or unwanted end; things—people—evaporate into thin air. We live in hope, that's all—and when that hope goes—*all* that hope, and in an instant—then everything else can go with it just like that—'He clicked his fingers, making a sound that echoed slightly in the high room.

He took an envelope from the same drawer that had held the magnifying glass. 'I made you copies of these.'

'What are they?'

'A few of the newspaper cuttings. Please, wait until you get home before you read them. They're nothing, really. A small and sorry tale on which most of the more recent "ghost" stories seem to be centred.'

The room contained half a dozen lamps, all with heavy shades, and he switched these on as the night finally enveloped us.

I was about to suggest that it was time for me to leave, when we were interrupted by someone knocking at the front door.

'I took the liberty of ordering you the local taxi,' he said.

He rose and led me back along the narrow hallway to the door. I felt unsteady on my feet, only realising the true extent of my drunkenness now that I was again upright and moving.

At the door, the driver walked immediately back to his car. 'Got your shopping, too,' he called to me, indicating the carrier bags on his back seat.

I thanked Alex Lister for the meal and his company.

He tapped the envelope of cuttings, now protruding from my pocket. 'Like I said, don't get your hopes up.'

I breathed deeply in the night air. It was another warm, still night. Lights showed in the buildings around me, but beyond these there was only the same impenetrable darkness in every direction.

I climbed into the taxi and when I looked back to the door I saw that Lister had already gone back inside—another retreat, it occurred to me, in his unhappy and directionless life of defeats.

Chapter Eight

The next day I slept late and woke shortly after noon. The door to the chalet was open and a soft breeze blew in off the sea and fluttered a newspaper on the table. It was the noise of this—a sound mimicking that of the distant waves—that had finally woken me. I had been dreaming of gulls, circling me where I walked on an endless dry plain, occasionally dropping and attacking me. And I knew as I fought off the birds that this assault was neither an accidental nor instinctive act, but that they were being directed in their aggression by someone walking far ahead of me in that empty place. The noise of the gently fluttering paper—once the waves—had become the sound of their beating wings in my dream.

I sat on the bed and remembered the previous evening. This time, the taxi driver had come from the road to the path and had delivered me and my groceries to the chalet door. He told me he was doing this as a favour to Mary Owen's mother, and that his opinion of the sand-blown track remained the same. He waited in his car, smoking, and with his radio filling the night's silence as I made two journeys with the bags.

I went to the doorway and looked out. A couple walked on the beach, throwing a ball for their small dog. Neither they nor the animal saw me watching them, or if they did then they paid me no attention and carried on walking. Despite the breeze, the surface of the sea was again perfectly calm, and blinding where it reflected the sun. A large flock of gulls floated on its surface, as silent and as motionless as the water itself.

Returning indoors, I unpacked my provisions and made coffee. Alex Lister's envelope lay on the floor beside my bed.

I opened this and slid out the few folded sheets it contained. Six newspaper reports concerning a lost child—most accounts preferred "missing"—and all of them disappointingly sparse, similar and inconclusive. Only one was from a national paper, the rest all local.

In September of 1962 a three-year-old child—a girl, Margaret Rose Jenner—had gone missing from the chalet in which she was living with her mother. The woman and child were alone, and lived permanently in their so-called seaside home. On the morning of Wednesday, the 29th of September, Rebecca Rose, the child's mother, had left the chalet and gone to the standpipe to collect their day's water, and upon her return, only a few minutes later, had found her daughter missing. Margaret Rose Jenner had been asleep in the bed she shared with her mother.

When a search of the chalet and its immediate surroundings did not reveal the child, Rebecca Jenner had solicited the help of her neighbours to extend the search.

An hour later, the child had still not been found, and so one of those neighbours had cycled to the village to call for the police. A few hours later, a wider search was set in motion, combing the inland fields and the beach for several miles in each direction. By the end of the day, the three-year-old girl had still not been found.

All of the reports printed the same photo of Mary Rose Jenner. She looked little more than a baby. Four of the six also printed a picture of her mother, who herself looked little more than a girl—she was twenty-one—and all of the accounts had something to say about the isolation of the place in which they lived, and about the impermanent nature of the buildings and the community of which Rebecca Jenner and her daughter had been a part.

I read all this in a matter of minutes, disappointed that there was no more—that the story being told was forever started but never finished. In only one of the reports—the national paper, the Daily Express for the first of October of that year—was there a picture of the place itself. The word "ramshackle" was used more than once to describe the home from which Mary Rose Jenner had gone missing.

The girl's father was said to be either "unknown" or "absent". Either way, he was not married to Rebecca Jenner, who said he did not even *know* of his daughter's existence. After police enquiries, it was accepted by all involved in searching for the girl that he had played no part in her disappearance.

I looked hard at the photograph, but I could distinguish nothing to show me which of the now derelict buildings the woman's home might once have been. It was a grey picture, and blurred, and the flimsy structure it portrayed seemed to blend into the background: shifting sand and terra firma, buildings and natural features, water, sand, road and land—everything seemed yet again of a piece in that place.

A spokesman for the local police said that the continuing search for Mary Rose Jenner would be properly planned and coordinated, and that he hoped for, and anticipated, a "happy outcome".

And that was where the story ended. Alex Lister might know more—though I doubted if that hoped-for "happy outcome" was ever realised—and perhaps it had only ever been his intention to whet my appetite for the story.

Before visiting him, I had hoped we might have enough shared interests in common to go on seeing each other regularly over the coming weeks, but even after only the few hours I had spent with him in his mausoleum of a home, I knew that this was unlikely to happen—that it was something neither of us would want or pursue. The whole evening, it seemed to me now, had been a test of endurance for him—a strange balance of his need to reveal *something* to me, and yet, ultimately, his reluctance to show me more than he actually had. He was there because it was the place where his beloved wife had suffered and died and then abandoned him. The place anchored and bound him. He was there because he could be nowhere else. His life, it occurred to me—his *existence*—had become intolerable to him. Everything that had once been bright and airy sunlight was now dark and confusing shadow to him; everything that had once been solid and sustaining to him was now dust and stale air. His home in that village was the only place he could live, and yet he had become a stranger and a recluse there, someone alienated and lost, without any real purpose or direction ahead of him.

And realising all this—though of course I had no true proof of *any* of it—I wondered if this existence might in some way be related to his curating—his ownership, almost—of all these small local stories. He had worked in the Museum and Archive service before his wife's illness and his own early retirement, and so perhaps all this gathering-in of the place's history was little more than some unstoppable momentum which continued to govern his life there, and which at least gave him some small purpose in the place.

I glanced outside and saw that the couple and their dog I'd seen earlier had turned and were now coming back towards me.

I took my coffee and sat on the sea wall. Their dog saw me first and ran to me and stood with its paws on the concrete beside me.

'He won't bite,' the man shouted to me—angrily, as though simply by sitting there I might have been encouraging the dog to do just that; as though I might even *deserve* to be bitten, dangling my bare legs and feet so close to the animal's mouth.

The woman called the dog back to them, but he refused to return, causing them both to come closer to me. I could sense their reluctance in every step they took.

'Lovely day,' I said when they were within talking distance.

'I suppose so,' the woman said.

The man concentrated on getting the dog to return to them, clearly frustrated that it showed more interest in me than in either of them.

'On holiday?' I asked them, prolonging their discomfort.

'What, here?' the woman said, pulling a face. 'Hardly. We're twenty miles away.' She named a lodge park I had never heard of.

'Like a caravan park?' I said.

'Caravan?' the man said. 'No, nothing at all like caravans. They're lodges. You know—*lodges*.'

'Not really,' I said. I knew exactly what the parks were.

'Built of wood,' the woman said. 'Logs. Like cabins, but more luxurious.'

'I see,' I said.

'Call them what you will,' the man said.

If the dog had gone back to them, they would have left me immediately.

'We have a veranda and a log-burning stove,' the woman said. 'Very cosy. It's our—what?—tenth visit to the place. We love it.' She looked beyond me as she spoke. 'And you?' she said. 'Are you'—she pulled a face and shrugged—'I don't know, working out here? Are they finally getting rid of these eyesores?'

'That's exactly it,' I said. 'The eyesores are finally going.'

'About time,' the man said. 'They should have bulldozed the lot of them decades ago and let the sand do its work. By rights, they should have taken down this wall, too.'

I pressed my palms against the wall's warm surface.

'But then the sea might come back in,' I said. I wondered if I hadn't put on a slight local accent.

'No "might" about it,' the man said. 'Best thing all round.'

They were both relieved when the dog finally lost interest in me and returned to them. The man quickly fastened a lead to its collar.

'Someone's taking over the abandoned holiday camp,' I said. 'Caravans. A funfair, swimming pools, that sort of thing. They're going to extend it from the road's end right up to here. This wall's going to be built up to three times its height. Last time I looked, they'd put in an application for twelve hundred caravans. I think there was even talk about lodges—or was it cabins?—in there, something of a high-end option. I think there are even plans for a cable car thing.' I finished my coffee and threw the dregs down on to the sand close to where they stood.

'But that's terrible,' the woman said. 'What, here? Right here?'

I motioned to the dilapidated chalets. 'Like you said—it's an eyesore, has been for donkey's years.' Now I was definitely using an accent.

'Well, that's the last time *we*'ll be coming,' the woman said, in a tone which suggested that the loss to the place was somehow greater than the loss of it to them.

'Sorry to be the bearer of bad news,' I said. 'Still, you're twenty miles away. Won't make that much difference, I don't suppose. And I daresay you have nice views from your cabin.'

'Lodge,' the woman said.

'Right. Sorry.'

She looked at me suspiciously for a moment and then signalled to her husband that she wanted to leave.

'A funfair, the lot,' I called after them. 'People will flock to the place.'

Neither of them answered me; neither of them even turned. They would quickly learn that everything I had just told them was a lie, that the impossible future of the place remained just that, and that all I had done had been to repeat the same unfounded and disappointing tales that had always been told of the place.

I watched them until they were tiny figures in the distance, and then I went back indoors.

Chapter Nine

The following night, and for the first time since my arrival, I slept badly. A succession of dreams ran one into the other—some of my life elsewhere and some of my life since arriving at the chalet. The disturbed birds featured again, as now did the mysterious woman. In one dream I was surrounded on the sand by a crowd of identical women, all of them dressed the same, all of them just out of my reach and focus, and all of them, for reasons unknown to me, professing to know me well, and making some angry demand of me. They shouted at me, and when they weren't shouting, they raised their faces and screamed and wailed into the sky above us. One moment I was standing in bright sunlight, the next it was pitch black, with neither the light of the moon and the stars nor the reflected metallic glow of the water to illuminate the scene. One moment I was sinking slowly into the soft, fine sand of the dunes, the next I was up to my chest in the water, the level rising with every lap of the tide. One moment the women were in the water with me, their heads barely above its surface, and the next they were all standing on the shore, beckoning and shouting out to me.

It was from this dream—trying to escape from these women, but being forced back towards them by the rising tide—that I finally woke into the darkness. I lay without moving, my eyes slowly focussing on the ceiling above me. The room seemed to contain a dying echo and I wondered if I had called out in my sleep. Perhaps it was this that had finally woken me.

It was another warm night, and my chest and face were filmed with a fine sweat. I swung my legs from the bed and sat for a moment to recover my lost balance. It was almost three, meaning I had slept for barely two hours.

The previous evening I had walked the inland paths to the rear of the empty camp site, and had then followed a drain which ran in a full circuit of the village until I was again facing the sea. The sun had fallen as I'd walked, but the summer light had never completely faded around me. And by then, after a fortnight in the place, I felt considerably more confident of my bearings and my route home. The full moon was bright, and wherever I stood in that once unfamiliar place, I was at least able to orientate myself by the shining sea.

It was almost ten by the time I'd returned to the chalet, after which I'd sat outside for an hour. The bottle of whisky had grown warm where I'd left it beneath my chair. Following my encounter with the couple and their dog, I had seen no one else for the rest of the day. It had been my intention to return Alex Lister's cuttings, but I could summon up neither the energy nor the enthusiasm for this so soon after our previous encounter.

Returning to the chalet, I had seen that the door was open, and I tried to remember if I'd left it like this upon my departure two hours earlier. I looked inside, but there was no indication that anyone had been there during my absence. My first thought was that perhaps Lister had come to see me—perhaps to add to the little he had so far revealed to me—but even as the thought occurred to me, I knew this was unlikely.

In one of my dreams of that night there had been a figure at my window—I couldn't tell if it was a man or a woman—looking in at me, and then swiftly moving away when I turned to face them. By the time I got to the door and looked outside, they had vanished completely. I imagined I could hear them somewhere in the surrounding darkness, running away from me, breathless and panting as they crossed the loose sand.

I doused my face in cold water and lit one of my lanterns. The smell of paraffin filled the air and I hung the contraption by the open window.

I had another drink, knowing from long experience that I would have difficulty falling back to sleep. I felt saddened that my dreaming turmoil, followed by this all too familiar sleeplessness, had returned to me. In the past, people had frequently told me that I looked exhausted or 'drawn', and my immediate response had been to tell them that in all probability I looked worse than I felt. I had a collection of full and unopened bottles of sleeping pills, mostly prescribed, somewhere amid the disarray of my bathroom.

I went outside and looked to the water. Unlike my dream, there were few stars and only a dim moon visible. The lights of two vessels showed on the horizon, both passing to the north. I rarely saw any ships during the daytime, and when I did I always wondered where they were bound, where they had come from and what they might be carrying.

The simple game reminded me of being a boy, standing with my father, who always took a pair of binoculars with him on our seaside holidays so that he might attempt to identify the flags or the letters painted on the passing ships' hulls and funnels. Before I was born, he had served in the Royal Navy, and his interest in the sea and everything upon it had never left him. He wore the binoculars on a strap around his neck and used them like a captain leading a convoy across dangerous waters. He would announce to me and my mother that some of the distant vessels, no more than low and indistinct shapes on the horizon, were too far outside of the designated shipping lanes—as though he was intimately familiar with where these might be—and he would announce their destinations and their cargoes with an equally convincing certainty. Usually, my mother indulged him in these fantasies and then raised her eyebrows to me, but for myself—and despite my inevitable feelings of guilt for not siding with her—I was always happy to go along with him and to extend his pleasure by asking him *how* he knew all these things. He told me he was an expert at deciphering those registration letters and numbers on the hulls and funnels, and in his binocular case he kept a small notebook and a stub of pencil with which to keep a record of everything he "sighted". My mother once gave him a pen to do this, but he had insisted that his few inches of carefully sharpened pencil—he was a man never without a pocket-knife—was the only tool for the job.

I remember him winking at me as he'd told her this. And then he had told her to ask *me*, her only son, if he wasn't right. Naturally—and thrilled to be a part of this rare intimacy between them—I had stoutly defended him until my father had laughed and announced that she stood no chance against the two of us. It was a rare intimacy all round.

All of this returned vividly to me as I stood and looked out at the passing lights. I felt a great and unexpected sadness at the sudden memory, and I tried to place it more accurately—where we had been, how old I had been, how old *they* had been, how long yet remained until their early deaths. But I was unsuccessful in this—I could have been anything between eight and sixteen—and though we visited only a few resorts on a regular basis, so similar were they, that it could have been any one of them, especially when standing on the shore and looking out to sea. It was that same east-facing coast, the sun always rising and falling ahead of us and behind us. I felt myself close to tears at everything so suddenly stirred within me. I still held my glass, and so I drained its contents and winced at the sharpness of the spirit.

Returning indoors half an hour later, I saw that the lantern had burned itself out. A small pool of leaked paraffin lay on the floor beneath it. The dry wick had burned to a charred ring, the acrid smell of which filled the room. I wiped up the spill and took down the lantern, taking it to the rear door and throwing it as far into the darkness as I could manage. I heard it land somewhere beyond the lean-to. I had half a dozen more to choose from.

In the dunes beyond, roosting birds gave occasional calls, unsettled perhaps by my presence there and by what I had just done.

I knew it was unlikely that I would fall back to sleep—the pattern was ingrained deep within me—but I returned to my flimsy bed and I laid on it.

By then, it was almost four, and the new day ahead was already brightening, the old one just passed nothing more than a slowly descending darkness in the west.

Chapter Ten

I next saw Alex Lister four days later. I had been walking the line of a raised bank further to the north—a rare direction for me—and upon my return I saw someone standing on the beach at the end of the road. My first thought was that it might again be the woman, but only a few yards closer and I was able to recognise Lister. He turned as I appeared in view and raised his hand to me. My immediate thought was that I wished he'd not seen me, that I had turned from the path and disappeared from his line of sight. Instead of this, I raised my hand and waved to him.

As I approached closer, he walked from the sea wall to the water's edge. The sea was again calm, only the darker sand and the wrack line of litter and feathers and desiccated seaweed showing where it had recently started to ebb.

'I called to see you,' I said, finally reaching him. I took out a handkerchief and wiped the sweat from my face and neck. I had finally returned to the village the previous day, but he had answered none of my knocks or calls. I had gone with the intention of returning his papers and finding out more about the missing child. I say that he had not answered me, rather than that I had found the house empty, because I was convinced that he had been present there upon my arrival, and that he had deliberately avoided responding to me. After a few minutes of this I had grown uncomfortable at the understanding and had come away from the house, deliberately not looking back at it as I'd crossed the small green to the shop. What would I have said to the man now if I'd seen him at one of the high, dark windows looking down at me?

'It's forecast to last for the next week at least,' he said, shielding his eyes to look up at the sun. 'The good weather.' He hesitated before going on. 'You knew I was in the house,' he said.

'I daresay—'

'Please, don't make excuses for me. I do enough of that myself these days. You came at a bad time, that's all. Sorry.'

'I wanted to return the clippings,' I said. 'I needn't have stayed.'

'Perhaps, but we would have gone through the usual awkward motions.'

I conceded to this in silence.

'Besides,' he said, 'you were probably more interested in finding out why I'd given you so little of the story.'

'I guessed most of the rest,' I said. 'I take it the lost girl never reappeared.'

'No. But the mother kept on coming. Until eventually even she stopped.'

'Did they assume the girl had drowned?'

'In the sea? Not very likely. She would have turned up. The tides and currents here are very predictable. No—the most likely scenario is that she fell into one of the deep and narrow dykes and that she drowned there. Some of those drains are ten feet deep, overhung, and half-filled with liquid mud even when the tide's out. It's happened before. It happens fairly regularly with the sheep occasionally grazed out here.'

'And the search?'

'For years afterwards there were reports of confessions and alleged sightings, but none of these ever amounted to anything.'

'But the mother never gave up hope?'

'Who knows? She left the place, but then came back here at every opportunity. Her chalet was condemned as unfit for habitation less than a year afterwards—the council was having one of its purges. She rented others. I think she might even have stayed in yours for a few summers. The council were determined to empty as many as possible; there were fewer and fewer of the places available each year. Back and back she came until—'

He stopped abruptly, looking down at the few inches of warm water that ran over his bare feet. His shoes sat where he had left them on the wall.

'Until—' I prompted him.

'Until one year she never appeared, never came.'

'Do you think she died?'

He shrugged. 'No one knows. Perhaps she died, or perhaps something else happened to her. Perhaps she just couldn't go on doing it anymore.'

'Or perhaps she just decided to get on with her life,' I suggested, knowing even as I said it how glib and uncaring the remark sounded.

He shook his head. 'That's something people say *today*. Back then no one was exhorted to "get on with their lives", to "move forward", to "get over it". No one told anyone else how to grieve, whether to keep things in or let them out. All this counselling and therapy—it's a disease in itself—telling people how to think and behave rather than just letting them come to their own understanding of things.'

'I suppose so,' I said, realising finally that he was talking as much about himself and his own lost wife as about the woman and her daughter.

'I could have given you ten times that number of articles to read,' he said.

'But it would have amounted to nothing more?'

He nodded. 'When she stopped coming back, people here said they were glad. They said she'd blighted the place. They, too, wanted her to "get on" with her life—only to do it as far away from here as possible. There was always talk of something or other about to happen here—something to revive its failing fortunes and bring it back to life—and the last thing they needed then was the grieving woman and all the horrors of her own life haunting the place and making everybody feel uncomfortable simply by coming back here.'

'And that's what happened?'

'More or less. Eventually. People reported her arrival here, and then her departure; they talked about where she was staying, where she was still searching. To begin with, she spoke to them, tried to solicit their help, but that soon stopped.'

'And afterwards?'

'I suppose she just learned to keep herself to herself, to avoid people. One time, apparently, she even accused the locals of keeping things from her. She went to the local paper and then made a complaint to the police. You can imagine how that all went down. We thought that when her own chalet—the one she'd lived in with her daughter—was condemned, that that might be an end to it all. The local vicar even offered to hold a service of remembrance for the lost girl. It would have been a big thing, back then. Not so much now, of course, where everyone is remembered and grieved over at every opportunity, even by complete strangers. Back then, it would have been something of a rarity. The odd man from the place was drowned at sea—either fishing or in the merchant marine out on some distant ocean—and there would be a ceremony—but that seemed only natural. Everybody here would have known him one way or another. The missing girl and her mother were a different thing entirely. Besides . . . ' And again he hesitated.

But this time I had already guessed what he was about to say.

'Did the mother ever actually accuse someone here of being involved in her daughter's disappearance?'

He smiled at this. 'She accused one man. And then another. Mostly she just went on accusing people of withholding information from her or of not helping her.'

'She actually accused men of abducting her daughter?'

'And worse.'

'And because the girl's body was never recovered—'

'The pointed finger and whispering and guessing just went on and on. Let's just say that she made herself very unpopular in the place. The local press had a field day with her. Big story, see? Every time there was an alleged sighting, it was front page news: the story never went away. The girl was allegedly spotted a hundred miles away only the day after she'd disappeared. And after that, she turned up at least once a year somewhere or other.'

'I suppose it sold papers.'

'Of course it did. And not only was it the kind of story that never really went away, but also one which always had a good enough reason to be told over and over again.'

Neither of us spoke for a moment. In the sky high above us, a jet left a perfectly straight and unbroken line of vapour across the whole of the sky.

'Do you think the mother thrived on the attention she was given?' I said eventually.

'It seems like that now. She was certainly indulged by the journalists wringing easy copy out of her. It was a missing child—who on earth was going to argue against doing whatever it might take to find the girl and return her to her mother?'

'I take it no arrests were ever made,' I said.

'None. A few local men were taken in for questioning—usually as a consequence of the woman's flailing accusations—but nothing ever came of it.'

'Except to breed more anger and resentment?'

'Except that.'

'What happened?'

He shrugged again. 'I suppose even the journalists finally lost interest. It was only ever a local story. Most of the papers were later either bought up or subsumed into conglomerates with their eyes on broader sales. I daresay the answer to "what happened?" is that they simply stopped approaching her at every new so-called development.'

'Leaving her to become her own ghost,' I said, mostly to myself.

'Sorry?' He looked down at the water rising around his ankles.

'So, in effect, she became her own ghost,' I said. 'She came back and people resented her and avoided her, and over time she did the same to them.'

'I suppose so,' he said. 'It would probably be nearer the truth to say that most people these days just want all uncertainty and confusion banished from their lives—they want explanations they can understand, accept and live with.'

'And not to be forever made to face something as dark and unsettling as the disappearance of a child?'

'Even *I* came to resent her continual reappearance and accusations,' he said.

'She can't have been the woman I saw,' I said. 'She'd be much older by now.'

'Sixty, at least,' he said. 'Besides, she hasn't shown her face in the place for decades.'

'The woman I saw was in her mid-twenties at the oldest. The age—'

'—she was when her daughter was lost.'

We both smiled at this.

'The ghost,' I said.

'First, the loss itself haunted the place, and then her reappearances haunted it.'

'She embodied a great deal,' I said.

'She certainly got *blamed* for a great deal. With every failed project and disappointed expectation, there would be some reference to the shadow she had cast over the place. Three years ago, a man walking the coastal path found a child's skull uncovered in the dunes after a gale. It turned out to be a thousand years old. You can imagine all the excitement *that* stirred up. A small team of archaeologists arrived. Naturally, I took an interest in the affair. I even vaguely knew the man in charge.'

'Did they find anything?'

'Nothing. Not even another bone. The land had changed a lot in those thousand years. By his reckoning, the skull came from a burial that had originally taken place five miles further inland.'

'Did the woman come back then?'

'Strangely enough, no. I doubt if she'd been back in the ten years before, either.'

'Suggesting she'd probably died in the meantime?'

'It's the best explanation. Besides, it would perhaps have been the final straw for her. Her own child is lost, and now, by some sheer fluke of the weather, here is the skull of another child—it was even considered to be that of a girl—who had died a thousand years earlier.'

After that we stood in silence for several minutes, listening to the noise of the retreating sea, its gentle scraping at our feet.

'I was on the stairs,' he said eventually. 'When you were at the door. Sitting on the stairs. I could see you through the coloured glass.'

'I don't mind,' I told him.

'I just get days when there seems absolutely no point to anything—none whatsoever—and when I wouldn't inflict myself on another living being.'

'You don't have to explain yourself,' I told him.

'No,' he said. 'I can see that.' He looked hard at me for a moment and then he walked out of the water and back on to the firm sand of the beach.

'Come for a drink,' I suggested.

He nodded, his face averted from me. He rubbed the soles of his feet against his calves to brush off the drying sand.

I went ahead of him to the chalet and waited for him at the vanished boundary of its lost garden.

Chapter Eleven

Three days after this encounter, I sprained my ankle while walking in the dunes. I was following a buried buttress of the concrete wall into the sand when this ended beneath me and I fell into a hollow there. At first I felt nothing, but when I rose and tried to stand, the pain started. I hopped to the nearest slope and settled into it. I studied my foot and saw that it was already starting to swell. I was at least half a mile from the chalet, and half that distance would be through the soft dunes. I prodded the swelling and then moved all of my toes. The pain subsided slightly and then returned when I tried to put any weight on the foot.

I had come into the dunes following the sketch Alex Lister had left me of where the ancient skull had been found and the disappointing excavation undertaken. But the place had clearly altered even over the intervening year and nothing on the simple plan now corresponded with any certainty with what I saw around me. I screwed the piece of paper into a ball and threw it away.

After resting, holding my injured foot into the sun, I rose and hopped several paces, following another of the vague paths through the dunes. The ground was soft and my progress slow. I found a piece of wood and used it to support myself and to keep my injured foot off the ground. I calculated that if I could return to the line of the buried wall, then I might follow this more easily back to the chalet. Every time I inadvertently caught my foot on the ground—I slipped and fell several times in the soft sand—I shouted out with the pain. Each time, this lasted only a few seconds before fading. The swelling on the side of my foot continued to rise and then to darken.

It took me ten minutes to return to the buried wall, where I rested my leg along the firm surface, and where I was finally able to cool down in the breeze off the sea.

It was as I lay like this, that I heard voices behind me. I sat upright and turned to look. I heard nothing more for a minute or two, and then the voices returned. I guessed they were children playing in the dunes I had just left behind me. And then I recognised the voice of Mary Owen. There was a boy and at least one other girl with her.

I waited for them to appear, pushing myself into a sitting position.

They came out of the dunes and then stopped abruptly upon seeing me ahead of them. Mary Owen, a boy, and the girl I had seen in the shop with her, Susan.

Mary was the first to see me, shielding her eyes to identify me where I sat and awaited them. The boy, I saw, carried a large plastic bottle of drink.

Mary spoke to them and then came to me alone.

'We were just walking in the dunes,' she said.

'As was I.'

'What for? Why?' She looked from me back to the others, beckoning them to join her. 'He was in the dunes,' she shouted to them, suggesting to me that perhaps she believed I had been watching them.

'Doing what?' the boy shouted back.

Mary looked at me.

'I learned about your ancient skull and I came to see where the dig had taken place.'

She seemed relieved by my answer. 'Oh, that? You couldn't see a thing a week after they'd all packed up and gone. Besides, it was ages ago.'

'Only a year.'

'Like I said—ages. They thought at first that it was the missing kid.'

'I know. Alex Lister told me.'

'Him again? And did he tell you he tried to stick his nose into what they were doing and got told to get lost?'

'I don't—'

'Thought not,' she said triumphantly. 'Thought he knew better than the man sent out to dig. He wanted them to go on looking, to dig here, there, everywhere.'

'And they didn't want to?'

'They said it was just a fluke, the thing turning up like that. They were only here for two days, and most of that was only on account of them thinking it might have been the missing girl. The night after it was found, they sent a copper in a Land Rover to sit there all night.'

'To stop—'

'To stop people with every right to go there from going there.' She climbed on to the wall beside me and looked out over the sea. Behind us, the two others came and sat further along. Mary told the boy who I was, and he said he already knew.

'How long have you been looking?' she asked me.

'Not long. I sprained my ankle.' I held up my swollen, discoloured foot for her to see.

She called for the boy to pass her the bottle he still carried. Susan took this from him and drank from it. I saw by the face she pulled that it contained more than cola.

Then Susan edged closer to the two of us.

Mary told her about my foot.

Susan looked down at it and said, 'That's going to hurt.'

'It already does,' I told her.

'I sprain *my* ankle all the time,' the boy said. 'Football, that sort of thing.'

'I did it in the dunes,' I told him.

'Give him a drink,' Susan told Mary, finally passing the bottle to her.

Mary took this, wiped the top on her t-shirt and passed it to me.

I swigged from it, talking several large mouthfuls.

'At least it'll dull the pain,' Mary said, and then laughed.

'I hope so,' I said, though in truth the pain had already eased since I'd been able to rest. I handed the bottle back to her and she swigged from it.

'Don't say anything to my mother,' she said. 'The drink.'

I guessed it was stolen from the shop. 'Of course not.'

'How long have you been out here now?' Susan asked me.

Mary answered for me.

'You seen the woman, then?' the boy asked me, but with little true interest in his voice.

'I saw *a* woman,' I said. 'But that was some time ago. Nothing since. She was probably just somebody walking on the beach.'

'Yeah, right,' he said. 'Here.'

'My dad said that the missing kid killed the holiday camp dead,' Susan said. 'He said they were going to find her when they started digging the foundations. Something like that.'

'Not very likely,' I said, offending her.

'How would you know? I was born and bred here. We all were.'

'I just meant—' I began to say.

'Everybody thinks that just because we live out here in the back of beyond, that we're thick,' the boy said.

'It isn't what *I* think,' I told him.

'No . . . well . . . ' he said. It was a concession of sorts.

'Besides,' Susan said, 'we've all seen her—the woman—at one time or another. Everybody round here has.'

'Wandering about the beach looking for her dead baby,' the boy added, grinning.

'I thought the girl was three years old,' I said.

'Baby, girl, much the same.'

Mary, who was now clearly angry at her exclusion from this exchange, said loudly, 'So he's seen somebody out here—so what? It's all just stories—something to give people a bit of a cheap thrill. To hear my mother talk about it, you'd think *she* was the only one who'd seen her, as though she had some special powers, or something.' She drank again from the bottle.

'I suppose so,' Susan said.

The boy dropped from the wall and crossed the sand-covered road. 'You going to be able to walk back?' He waved in the direction of the chalets.

'I'm going to try,' I told him.

'You might need an x-ray,' Susan said.

'I hope not.' I lightly touched the swelling, but felt little. 'I think it's settling down.'

Mary dropped from the wall and stood in front of me. She raised my foot and examined it more closely. 'Move your toes,' she said.

I did this.

'Nothing broken,' she said, guessing at what I already knew. She traced the outline of the tender flesh with her forefinger, telling me to shout out when this hurt. Only when she prodded at the centre of the swelling did I finally feel anything.

'Ouch,' I said.

'"Ouch"? Who says "Ouch" anymore?' she said, smiling.

'Men who sprain their ankles,' I said.

'If you *did* need an x-ray, I could get my mother to send the taxi. The hospital's twenty miles away, further.'

'So it would probably cost me an arm and a leg just to save a foot,' I said.

She shook her head at the feeble joke.

Only the boy laughed, and then repeated the remark several times.

'Ignore him,' Mary told me.

'*We* usually do,' Susan added.

After several more minutes of resting, and another round of the drink, I told them that I felt able to continue walking.

Susan gave me my stick. The pain of the first few steps made me wince and again shout out with the pain. A dozen further steps and I knew how best to angle my foot to prevent any jarring.

'Come and help him,' Mary shouted to the boy.

'*You* help him,' he shouted back. 'You're the one who—'

'You're the strongest,' she shouted. 'At least that's what you're always telling everybody.'

He came to me reluctantly and told me to put my arm around his shoulders. Susan went to the other side of me and held my forearm, steadying my balance as I hopped and pushed my way forwards on the stick.

Stopping every few paces, we made good progress, certainly better than I would have made alone. I pointed out the chalet when it came into view ahead of us. The wicker chair still sat at the open door.

In ten minutes we reached our destination.

'You never know,' the boy said, helping manoeuvre me into the chair, 'you might have done more damage than you know—internal, that sort of thing—you might fall asleep tonight and then die in your sleep without ever realising it.'

'It's a sobering thought,' I said, sharing a smile with Mary.

'Ignore him,' she told me. 'He's always saying that sort of thing.' She put a cushion beneath me and then held my arm as I finally lowered myself into the chair.

'No—you're missing my point,' the boy insisted. 'What I'm saying is that you might die out here and then lie undiscovered and stuff until somebody from outside actually comes looking for you.'

'And then *I*'d be your next ghost.'

'Exactly,' he said excitedly. 'Exactly. See—*he* knows what I'm saying.' He took the bottle from Susan and drank from it. 'At least then *we*'d all know the true story of what happened. Not like all this other rubbish.'

Mary went into the chalet and came out with a plastic bowl. She told the boy to go to the tap and fill it.

'What for?' he said.

'Guess.'

'Oh, right,' he said. He took the bowl from her and walked slowly to the tap.

When he returned, I lowered my foot into the water and called out again at the shock of this. Within seconds, the pain was numbed.

The three of them waited with me a further hour, exploring the chalet and its close surroundings, telling me about their lives in the place and what lay ahead of them. The boy was starting college in a month's time, and Susan said her sister worked as a nanny in London and had promised to find her similar work there. Only Mary Owen, it seemed, had made no definite plans to leave, and I knew better than to ask her about this in front of these others.

After an hour, they left along an invisible path alongside the chalet—the quickest way back to the village, the boy said—telling me they'd see me again.

'Unless I die first,' I said.

'You won't die,' Mary told me.

'He might.' Only the boy still had any enthusiasm for the idea.

I could hear their voices long after they were lost to my sight. And when these finally faded, there was again only the noise of the water and the breeze in the grass.

Chapter Twelve

I was woken much later that night by a sound close by the chalet. My immediate thought was that another bird had landed on the roof above me. This happened frequently, but seldom failed to surprise me, especially in the darkness.

I lay without moving, listening for the sound of footsteps above me. But these never came. My ankle still caused me pain. I had fallen asleep with my injured foot hanging out of the bed, but when I woke it was back on the thin mattress and aching again. Ever since the departure of Mary Owen and her friends, I had been taking painkillers.

I was about to take two more of these when I heard the noise again. This time, I was convinced that someone was outside, close by, moving around the chalet.

I looked at my watch and saw that it was just after three, the heart of that summer's night. The sky was seldom truly dark those days, and I could already see the brighter sky in the east. It was over six weeks past the height of the summer, but this faint light still forever showed on the low horizon.

I lay perfectly still and continued listening. I heard *something*, but still could not say for certain what this was—something moving, it struck me; footsteps in the sandy soil hardly sounded at all. This noise sounded like something actually brushing against the chalet, moving back and forth from the walls. It was at the rear of the building, perhaps beside the small lean-to. Anything or anyone going in there would be sure to disturb something or other, and I could then be more certain in my guessing. But there was nothing.

It then occurred to me that, in all likelihood, what I was listening to was a fox scavenging over the empty land, or possibly a gull moving from one roost to another. I had thrown all my waste into a lidless bin beside the outhouse, so perhaps this had attracted the creatures. It also occurred to me that my reasoning was being distorted by the painkillers and the alcohol I had consumed over the past twelve hours.

For a further five minutes there was only silence, and then I heard a definite knock against the side wall. I almost called out at hearing this, but held my breath and waited.

A moment later, and as I tried to focus on where the knock had actually sounded a shape—a shadow, an outline—passed across the chalet's small front window, left to right, neither stopping nor pausing, and in a swift and fluid motion. The open door stood only a yard away, and I waited for whoever had passed the window—I was convinced now that it was a person rather than an animal or bird—to appear there. But even as I waited and watched, I knew that whoever might be there—whoever had passed the window—would already have passed the doorway too and be on the far side of it by now. Five seconds had passed, less, but the distance between the window and the door would have taken only half that time. Had I been so concerned with the outline at the window that I had missed it at the doorway? Or had whoever it was stopped after passing in front of the window and was now waiting against the wall rather than reveal themselves to me at the door? Did whoever it might be even know I was inside the chalet? Was *I* about to become an even bigger surprise to whoever was outside than they had already been to me?

I waited a further minute, but neither saw nor heard anything more. I listened intently in case I might hear someone breathing. I searched for signs of breath in the doorway. I looked hard at the wall to try and detect if anyone now hiding outside was leaning against it. But I still saw and heard nothing, and after a further few minutes of waiting, I began to doubt what I might or might not have seen at the window. For all I knew, it might only have been the shadow of a cloud over the moon. The moon was certainly in the right place for this to have happened; I could even see it through the door. Or it might have been the shape or shadow of a bird flying close by and low. I had frequently watched the gulls in the night, seeing what abstract and vivid and un-birdlike shapes, configurations and patterns they made as they came and went in the darkness.

I felt my foot begin to throb where it touched the metal frame of the bed. The bowl of water lay beside me, most of it now spilled on the boards of the floor. I considered taking off my simple bandage and soaking my foot again, but decided against this. There had been no further noise for at least ten minutes.

Eventually—and having convinced myself that the painkillers and alcohol *were* the cause of what I had or hadn't seen and heard—I swung myself into a sitting position, hearing the bed creak beneath me. I cursed as I caught my foot against the bowl. The painkillers and whisky still sat on the table close at hand. I took several tablets and poured myself a drink. If there *was* anyone hiding outside, then they would be in no doubt now that the place was occupied.

Waiting until I felt able to stand, I pushed myself up and went to the door. There was no one there. I was as alone as I had always been and there was no sign whatsoever of anyone or anything close by. The wicker chair sat where I had left it. The air was still, but above me the night clouds were drifting in a higher wind, moving across the face of a full moon just as I had imagined. Birds roosted on the wall beyond the road. Most were unaware of my arrival in the doorway, but those closest to me shuffled nervously at my appearance before settling again.

I searched the ground for footprints and remembered my earlier visitors. I went to the chair and lowered myself into it, raising my leg on to the crate Mary Owen had put there for me. The pain in my ankle seemed to ease. I leaned back and closed my eyes. Whatever I had heard was long gone by then, and had been no threat whatsoever to me.

And it was as I finally felt myself relax like this that I again heard something in the darkness—much further away this time, beyond the end of the road—and something which was either a door swinging on its hinges or someone opening and then closing that door. I searched in the direction of this new sound, but saw nothing. Everything seemed to possess a faint echo at that time of night, and because of the stillness and the absence of any other sound, locating anything with any accuracy was difficult.

I waited where I sat, watching the road in both directions. The shadows of the drifting clouds came and went, and when they moved directly over me I expected to feel their chill, but of course there was nothing; they shielded the moon from me, not the sun. My ears attuned themselves to the faint noise of the sea. I searched the horizon for the distant lights of other passing ships, but there was nothing. I tried to remember how many days I had been there—how many nights—but could only guess within a day or two.

I convinced myself I was finally detaching myself from the broken pattern and routine of my former life, and that it was something I should have done much sooner. And then I told myself that the drink and painkillers were still doing their work in shaping my scattered, confused thoughts. I would soon enough return to my old life; it would soon enough reclaim me, and I would soon enough—in one way or another—take up again where I had left off upon coming here. Everything that had frayed and parted would be brought back together, reconnected, however tentatively, and would then be made strong again. I was the same man I had always been, and it was the same world in which I still lived. This was a solitary season of a single year in a life of years. Everything remained the same and continued along its same steady and predictable course. What was it they said? That even the far and distant future would always contain the past; and that the past—however completely we might *imagine* we were keeping it behind us—forever clothed us in the present.

This tangle of confused thoughts and reasoning filled my mind until, in the silence of the dying night, I fell back to sleep where I sat.

Chapter Thirteen

I spent the following week almost entirely alone. The pain from my ankle slowly eased, and after two days I was able to walk without using a stick. I kept the bandage on, and each day I soaked my bruised foot in cold water and checked on the progress of the swelling. The bruising remained for longer than I expected, but that too gradually faded.

On the third morning of my isolation, I woke to find another box of groceries and a note from Mary Owen saying that she had arrived while I was asleep and that she had been unable to stay.

Following my disturbed night, I was again sleeping well, and it was almost one in the afternoon before I discovered the groceries. I went outside in the hope of seeing the girl, but both the road and the beach were deserted.

Overall, there were fewer people on the beach than previously, and this surprised me. I had imagined upon first arriving there that it would have been a popular part of the coast for walkers, but this clearly wasn't the case. I had even anticipated that families might come from nearby towns to spend whole days on the beach. But perhaps they had once come and were now better entertained elsewhere. Or perhaps the lack of facilities and the general air of neglect and abandonment that hung over the place deterred them from returning.

On the same afternoon I found the groceries, I saw two men—a father and his son was my first thought—walking along the water's edge. I stood on the wall, and when they saw me they diverted their course towards me.

'Seen anything?' the man asked me.

'Seen?'

'Sorry. Thought you were bird-watching.' He tapped the binoculars hanging at his chest. 'That's us—bird-watching. Supposed to be a Sabine gull somewhere around here. Got a message a couple of hours ago. Thought we'd try our luck.'

His son nodded vigorously at everything the man said. The boy remained expressionless and watched us both closely, turning his head from one to the other depending on who was speaking.

'I'm David. This is Andrew,' the man said.

I shook his hand.

The boy backed away from the gesture.

I told them I wouldn't know a Sabine gull from a pelican.

The man laughed and then repeated what I'd said to his son. Then the boy left us and returned to the water's edge.

'He's happy just to be walking and looking,' the man said to me, his eyes following his son, who took out his own binoculars and scanned the empty sea.

'Holidaying?' the man said to me, searching behind me. It seemed a strange word to me.

'Just staying a few weeks.' I motioned to the chalet.

'Last of the few, eh?'

'It looks that way.'

He searched along the line of chalets. 'All be gone this time next year.'

'It's news to me,' I said.

'You must have read the papers. The nature reserve? No? Ten miles in either direction.' He named two places I hadn't heard of. 'Flatten that lot'—he motioned again to the chalets—'and cart away the wreckage. And after that, they'll get rid of the wall. Two or three years down the line and the place will be unrecognisable. Let the sea back in, see? Government policy. The Environment Agency.'

'And all for the better?' I said absently.

'What else? Sorry. You own the chalet?'

'Friend,' I said.

'Right, well, you'll know all this better than I do.'

'Not really,' I said.

He looked at me as though I might have been lying to him; or perhaps trying to draw something out of him that, for some reason or other, he ought not to reveal to me. He looked back to his son, who was now writing in a pad.

'He lists everything. And I mean everything. Autism. On top of everything else. You can't imagine.'

'He seems content enough,' I said, immediately regretting the glib and condescending remark.

'Oh, he's that, all right. I sometimes wonder if that isn't half the problem.' He shook his head, as though he too regretted what he'd just said. 'He's his mother's world. Only child. Came along when we'd all but given up—well, you can imagine.'

'I suppose so,' I said. I suddenly wanted him to go back to the boy at the water's edge, and for the pair of them to carry on walking away from me and never to return.

After a moment's awkward silence, he said, 'They're saying the weather's going to break soon.'

'They're always saying *something* about it. If it's good, it's going to get worse; if it's bad, it's going to get better.'

And again he looked at me as though I had either tricked or insulted him.

At the sea's edge, his son now stood with the water coming over his shoes. The man saw this and shouted to him, leaving me to run down the slope. He reached the boy and pulled him back on to the dry sand. His son showed him what he'd just written in his pad and the man stood and read this, exclaiming with delight and surprise at everything he saw. After a minute of this, he looked back to where I still stood and watched them. He said something to the boy and the boy waved at me. I waved back and the pair of them continued their walk.

I remained outside for the rest of the day. I read for a while, and after that—and despite my previous long night's sleep—I slept in the sun.

I now inhabited a boundless emptiness upon which no real order or routine was imposed, and within which no real demands were made of me. I occasionally stayed awake through most of the night, and I sometimes slept intermittently through the day. My every exertion—few and brief though these now were on account of my ankle—seemed to tire me. Sometimes, I craved that emptiness and freedom, and at other times I craved purpose and company. 'Purpose' is too imprecise—too grand a notion, even—but I can think of no other word. And on the few occasions—especially during the week of my recuperation—when strangers did appear, I wanted only to be left alone again. I lived an aimless existence—perhaps one to be envied, perhaps pitied. I made no true plans beyond the fluid passing of my days. I tried to look neither backwards nor forwards. My days and nights came to seem less to me than the coming and going of the tide.

The land, and all its edges and junctions, was an unreliable and insubstantial place, and the sea alone, it seemed to me now, possessed strength, predictability and energy.

I slept again, and when I next woke, the day's light was fading around me. Here, too, I had become adept at gauging the time by this darkening and brightening of the sky, and by the angle, depth and length of the shadows which surrounded me. What was light became dark; what was warm grew cold. I could choose to move in accordance with these changes, or I could choose to submit myself to them. My hair and clothes filled with sand. I angled my face to cooling breezes. I forever felt the taste of salt on my lips, and in turn it forever reminded me of something vital now completely lost to me, of blood almost.

Chapter Fourteen

Mary Owen returned to the chalet three days later. She came in to me without knocking and sat beside me where I slept. It was mid-afternoon and I had been both awake and sleeping since the dawn.

'You survived, then,' she said as I finally woke and looked at her where she sat.

'I suppose so.'

She indicated the new groceries she had brought for me. 'My mother says she needs something on account.' The request bore no urgency. She looked at the room around her.

'Are the others with you?' I said. I swung my legs from the bed and straightened my shirt.

'Susan's already gone,' she said. 'Off to her fantastic new life in London.'

'And—?' I tried to remember if I had ever known the boy's name.

'Ian,' she said. 'He reckons all this coming out here is just a waste of time. Something for kids. There's an open day at some college or other. He's gone to that. I was supposed to be going with him . . . '

'But?'

'But what? No point if I'm going to be stuck out here. It's twenty miles each way. He'll manage it for a term, if that.'

It seemed a ridiculous argument, not even that.

'You could at least see what they have to offer,' I suggested.

'I *could*,' she said. She rose from the table and went to the doorway. 'You've let that garden go,' she said, laughing.

'I doubt if it even qualifies for the name any more,' I said. 'Apparently, this time next year, you won't even know there was a *chalet* here.' I tried to remember what else the bird-watching man had told me.

'The nature reserve?' she said dismissively. 'They've been talking about that for years,' she said. Another half-turned page in the unhappy history of the place.

I went to join her and we went outside and sat together in the afternoon sun.

'You should have gone to hospital, and then gone home,' she said, examining my foot, where both the swelling and the bruising had by then almost completely faded.

'Perhaps,' I conceded.

'Susan says she has no intention of ever coming back here, not even at Christmas.'

'London's only a couple of hours away,' I said.

'You think so?'

It was pointless to argue with her.

'Anyone been to see you?' she said after a long silence.

'No one. I thought Alex Lister might come.'

She shrugged at this. 'He usually keeps himself to himself.'

I offered her a drink and she said she wanted only water, which I fetched for her.

'What did you think you'd find—looking where they found the skull?' she asked me.

'Nothing. Not really. I just wanted to see where it was.'

'There are still people here who think it was all a cover-up—that it really was the skull of the missing girl, and that the police and the authorities covered everything up by pretending it was much older.'

'Unlikely,' I said. 'To what end?'

'I'm not saying *I* believe it,' she said.

'There'd have been considerably more interest in the place if it *had* belonged to the missing girl,' I said.

'I know. It's the same people who say the mother put a curse on the place.'

I resisted laughing at the word and all it implied.

'They think she blighted the place by losing her daughter here,' I said. 'That's all. And then that she went on blighting it by returning here and forever stirring everything up.'

'I suppose so,' she said. 'My mother says they knock down the homes of murderers, people like that—knock them down, level the land and then cart everything away.'

'And she believes that something similar ought to have been done here, with the chalet?'

She shrugged. 'She's as ridiculous as the rest of them. I doubt if she even knows which chalet it was. Not after all this time, not after most of them started falling down of their own accord anyway.'

'Do *you*?' I said. 'Know which chalet it was, is?'

'What's left of it,' she said. She turned away from me as she spoke.

Ever since my sighting of the distant woman, I had associated her with a particular building, beyond the road's lost terminus, and corresponding with the end of the sea wall. It remained a more substantial structure than most of those still around it. It had no door—nothing to bang in the breeze in the middle of the night—and the glass had long since gone from its windows. But its walls at least remained upright and its roof mostly intact. Closer to, of course, it had revealed itself to be considerably more decrepit and completely uninhabitable. The sand which now surrounded it also filled its exposed interior at least a foot deep, and beyond the building, the encroaching dunes had long since covered its own lost garden and already stretched to the fields beyond.

I told her where I had explored, and she waited a moment before answering me. 'That's not it,' she said. 'It's further from the wall's end. You can't miss it on account of all the crosses.'

'Crosses?' I wondered if this was a test.

'On the wall. Crosses carved in the wood. Hundreds of them.' She took out her phone, worked at it for a few seconds and then showed me a picture. 'We used to pretend it was a way of keeping the woman—her ghost or whatever—in the place.'

The photograph showed a dark wooden wall into which countless small and simple crosses had been carved, along with a variety of other graffiti—names and initials, mostly—much of this barely discernible, but a few here and there more recently carved and still visible.

'We used to say that if you made a cross on the wall each time you went past the place—more often than not we just used stones—then you'd keep her away from you. Some people made crosses out of pebbles on the ground all around the place.' She took the phone back from me and found another picture.

'Do people still do it?' I asked her.

'Draw the crosses? I doubt it. No need. Besides, we were kids.'

I guessed then that it was something she still did if she ever returned to the chalet.

'When we were kids, we'd come out here every day in the summer. It was just our way—I don't know—'

'Of keeping yourselves safe? Some kind of insurance?'

'I suppose so.' She smiled at something. 'One time, we recorded Susan's baby sister crying, and came out here with a player.'

'To scare people?'

'Other kids, mostly. And once we knew some reporter had turned up on the anniversary of the girl's disappearance.'

'What happened?'

'We kept a long way from him. It was late—nine, ten o'clock.'

'In the summer?'

She nodded. 'Like now. We hid on the far side of the dunes, switched on the recording and then turned it up and down. At first we weren't even sure if he'd heard it. And then he turned to look where we were hiding. We switched it off straight away. He left after that—back to where he'd left his car on the road. The next week the local rag was full of it—a ghostly crying baby to go with the ghostly wailing woman.'

'Did anyone ever find out what you'd done?'

'A few. I think someone even wrote to the paper to tell them what had probably happened. It might even have been old man Lister.'

'And?'

'And what? Nothing happened. Susan said it was because the ghost story was better than anything else they had. You'd be surprised how many people wrote in afterwards to say that *they'd* heard the crying baby, too.'

'I suppose that's how it works,' I said.

'That's *definitely* how it works.' She shielded her eyes to search the empty beach and the sea. 'My mother's talking again about shutting up the shop. The landlord wants to put the rent up and she can't afford it.'

'What will she do instead?'

She shrugged again. 'Knowing her, she'll just sit and rot. Like everybody else here.'

And you with her? I thought. 'And you?'

'Who knows?'

'You could—'

'There are thousands of things I *could* do,' she said, her voice rising.

I knew better than either to pursue the matter or to apologise to her, and so we sat in silence for a further few minutes until this sudden tension was slowly released. We watched a flock of terns twist and turn in perfectly synchronised manoeuvres out over the sea, looking more like smoke than living creatures, flickering and thinning as they flew, and then bunching and spreading out to near-invisibility as they passed us by over the water.

Chapter Fifteen

Three days later, when my foot was finally fully recovered, and I felt confident of making the journey, I returned to see Alex Lister.

As I crossed the small green to his home, I was conscious of Mary Owen's mother watching me from the doorway of her shop. I called to her, but if she heard me, she didn't answer me.

I waited at Alex Lister's door, peering through the opaque glass, but knowing even as I looked that I would see only the darkness inside. I knocked and waited. Turning, I saw that the woman in the doorway had been joined by another—both of them now more interested in me than whatever else they might have had to discuss. There was no response to my knock, and after a minute I tried again. Again, there was no response. Unlike my previous unsuccessful visit, when I'd guessed he had been in the house and was deliberately avoiding me—and to which he'd admitted at our last encounter—I sensed on this occasion that the house was indeed empty, that Alex Lister was elsewhere, and that my effort to see him had been a wasted one.

I retraced my steps across the road. I wasn't too disappointed that I had missed the man. I had little true idea of why I had returned to see him, other, perhaps, than to tell him that I had decided to leave the place. Perhaps he would have shown me more of his informal archive, perhaps not. Perhaps a new facet of the sorry tale might have been revealed to me, perhaps not. Or perhaps he would have finally revealed to me what, other than the inertia following the death of his wife, still kept *him* there. This last, I knew, was the least likely of all.

I came close to the two women, who braced themselves at my approach. Mary Owen's mother was smoking, and she threw down the last of her cigarette and rubbed it out with her foot as I arrived beside them.

'Come to settle up?' she asked me.

'Of course. I was hoping to see . . . ' I motioned over my shoulder. 'I don't suppose you know—'

'If he's out?' She pursed her lips.

'You never know with that one,' the other woman said. 'Keeps himself to himself.' She looked at the house. 'I can tell you one thing, though—he's let that place get on top of him.'

I turned to look at the overgrown front garden, at the peeling paint on the door and window frames, and at the grass growing the full length of the high gutter.

'I daresay . . . ' I said, uncertain of what to add.

Mary Owen's mother took several pieces of paper from her pocket, searched through them and then handed one to me. It was my bill—not itemised reckoning, merely a figure written in pencil. It was beyond me to ask for any breakdown of this; whatever I said would suggest suspicion to her—disbelief on my part, fraud on hers.

'It's all tallied up inside,' she said, as though reading my thoughts.

'Of course,' I said. 'I'm grateful for everything you've sent.' I took out my wallet and paid her.

'I heard about your foot,' she said.

I wondered what else her daughter had told her.

'Yes, well . . . '

'You'll be running low again,' she said.

I admitted that I was, but that I would be leaving soon and would need less than previously.

'Do you need anything in particular?'

'Same as before,' I said. 'Mary knows.'

'Oh, I'm sure she does. Knows everything, that one. And what she doesn't know she'll make up without a moment's thought for the consequences.'

The other woman smiled to herself and looked away from us.

I was uncertain what—if anything—had been meant by the remark, and so I said nothing.

'Right . . . ' I said eventually. 'I ought to be getting back.' I took several steps away from them.

'You can check everything on your bill against what I've sent out,' Mary Owen's mother said. She seemed surprised now that I had paid without asking for details.

'No need. Really,' I said. I continued walking away from them, skirting the open space until I came to the path which ran alongside Alex Lister's home back out into the fields.

I was glad to emerge from the cool and shade of this alleyway and return to the warmth of the afternoon. The unseen track ahead of me was by then a familiar one and I was confident of my return to the chalet in under an hour.

Arriving at the first hedge, I turned towards a drain and climbed a few feet up onto its low embankment. From there, I could look forward over the open expanse of land leading to the sea, and back to the rear of the village houses and their gardens.

I sought out Alex Lister's distant home and looked hard at its windows, all of them reflecting the pale, empty sky above. Even if I had seen him there, he would never have identified me at that distance. I waited where I stood for several minutes, conscious that I would soon return to the life I had left behind me, and that, in all likelihood, I might never see him again. Inexplicably, the realisation saddened me, but only briefly, and I resumed walking. I swatted swarms of small flies from my face as I followed the line of the water.

I walked to the junction of the path leading to the coast road, and prior to coming down from this slight elevation, I looked back for a final time.

And this time—and against all expectation—I saw a figure standing at the centre of Alex Lister's garden. Him, presumably—standing perfectly still for a moment and then vigorously pacing back and forth. My first thought was that he had regretted having avoided me earlier and that he had now come outside to somehow call or signal to me to return to him. Perhaps he might even want to apologise to me for not having come out to me after so long an absence.

But I knew as I watched the distant, pacing figure that he had no intention whatsoever of trying to contact me and that he was as oblivious to my distant, watching presence as he had been to me earlier at his door.

I waited and watched for a few minutes longer, after which I descended the few steps from the embankment and was no longer able to see him. In fact I was now no longer certain which of the walls or hedges surrounded his own garden, and so I turned my back on the place and continued walking.

It soon became clear to me that I had overestimated the strength of my injured foot, and as I crossed the hard ground of the baked fields I felt the return of the gentle throbbing sensation I had endured for the previous week—not pain, exactly, merely a feeling to remind me that some weakness still remained.

I walked more slowly and rested more often, soon coming within sight of the sea road, and then the chalets, and then the sea itself. I felt relieved to be on this final, familiar stretch.

It had been my intention upon setting out to return via the derelict chalet scribbled and gouged with its graffiti and crosses, but I decided instead to go straight home and rest my foot.

I reached the chalet twenty minutes later and fell into the chair at the doorway, supporting my foot and looking out over the empty beach, finally relieved that I no longer needed to walk anywhere.

I again fell asleep where I sat, the sun on my face, and when I woke I was immersed in shadow. It seemed unbelievable to me, but I had slept for almost six hours. The gulls made their usual distant clamour out over the water, and perhaps this was what had woken me. I watched them for a while before going indoors. I lit two of my lanterns, and a small fire in the cast iron stove, warming my hands as first the kindling, and then the small pieces of grey driftwood burned. I knew by then which of these to choose—those which had fully dried, and which didn't forever crackle and spit with the salt which lay through their grain. I poured myself a drink.

Ten days, ten more dawns and sunsets, ten more days of formless routine and wandering and the rising and falling tides.

It occurred to me as I sat at the stove that if either Lister's or Mary Owen's predictions came true, then, in all likelihood, I would be the chalet's final occupier—the final inhabitant, in fact, of that whole small colony of lost homes and lives, and I drank a toast to the realisation and to everyone who had ever been there before me.

And after that, I slept again, and this time when I woke it was to find myself beside a cold stove and an empty bottle, and sitting alone in the darkness and the silence at the heart of yet another warm and airless night.

Chapter Sixteen

The following morning, my foot again feeling much stronger, I returned to the chalet Mary Owen had pointed out to me on her phone and examined for the first time its wall of crosses and graffiti. These reminded me both of the beribboned tokens people hung from trees and of mawkish roadside bouquets.

Every mark and letter on the wall might have been a clue to something—to whatever past and momentous event still gave the place its resonance—but beyond the much-embellished story of the woman and her lost child, I still had no real idea what that something might be. It was a tale of loss built on rumour and whispers, and something which only unravelled or evaporated further with each excited retelling.

As I had guessed from the photo, some of the marks were clearly more recent than others—entwined initials, the scrawl of the lovelorn and the desperate—whereas others might have been there for decades, weathered and darkened and scrubbed away by the wind and the spray and the sand. I wondered who had drawn the first of the simple crosses—what this had signified to them, what message the mark was intended to deliver to others coming to the place—and when these had started to multiply. It was clear to me that the symbols and the distant event were connected, but it was a simple connection to make and it signified little else. I saw the same initials repeated, in various combinations. I saw "MO", which I took to be Mary Owen. She was there four times, and each time with someone else. Small crosses filled most of the empty spaces on the tilted wall, simple additions to the canvas. Nails and screws protruded here and there, and I wondered what might once have been attached to these—dead gulls, perhaps, or other pieces of flotsam retrieved from the wrack.

I searched the ground around the ruined building for sign of the crosses composed of pebbles Mary Owen had spoken of, but found nothing in the sandy soil.

Disappointed by what little had been revealed to me, I left the chalet and returned to my own.

As I approached this, I saw a rare car coming slowly along the road. This stopped and then turned at the stand-pipe and I saw that it was a police car. The driver pulled to the side of the road and got out. He saw me in the distance ahead of him and waved to me. I waved back and continued to my chalet, where he finally joined me.

He was a young man, burdened with equipment which hung from his belt, chest and arms.

'I'm Special Constable Cook,' he told me.

'From the village?'

'From the Eastleigh Station.'

I offered him a seat, indicating my bandaged foot.

'You've injured yourself,' he said.

'Just a sprain.'

I waited for him to tell me why he was there.

Instead, he asked me if he could look inside the chalet, and then went to the open doorway, holding the frame on each side of him, almost as though bracing himself against what he might find inside.

He turned back to me. 'Would you mind telling me where you've been?' It seemed a strange question to ask in that place.

'To look at another of the chalets,' I said. I pointed towards the far end of the road.

'Oh? For any specific purpose?'

'Just to look,' I said. 'It's supposed to be where a woman lost her daughter fifty years ago?'

He pursed his lips and slowly shook his head. 'News to me,' he said. 'I live in Eastleigh. Besides, fifty years?'

'It's a local tale,' I said. 'A woman staying in one of the chalets lost her three-year-old daughter and the girl was never found.'

'And so you were looking why? If you don't mind me asking.'

'Just to satisfy my curiosity, I suppose,' I said, knowing it was the simple truth, but also how unconvincing this sounded.

'Right.' After a pause, he said. 'Can you identify yourself for me, please, sir.'

'Identify?'

'Driving licence, credit card, something of that nature.'

I showed him my wallet and all it contained.

'That's fine,' he said. 'Sorry. It's just that you sometimes find yourself talking to the wrong person completely.'

Which meant what? That it was me, specifically, he had come to see?

'And is the chalet yours?' He looked around him as he spoke.

'It belongs to a friend of mine. He let me have it for a few weeks. A kind of holiday.'

He took a notebook from his pocket and opened it. 'According to my information, you've been here well over a month now. Would that be correct?'

I told him how long I'd been there and how much longer I intended staying.

'Any particular reason for your departure?'

'Not really,' I said, irritated by all these half-questions and half-accusations. 'I had no real idea of how long I was going to stay when I arrived. If you let me know what all this is about, I can give you the owner's number. Whatever anyone might have told you, I *am* entitled to be here.'

'Really, there's no need to explain yourself, sir.' He held up his palms to me. And then he smiled at me. 'Besides, it's nothing like that. I doubt they'd send me all the way out here just for something like that, for something so . . . so . . .'

I offered him a glass of water and he took it.

‘So why *are* you here?’ I asked him.

‘I understand you’re acquainted with Alex Lister. A witness says you were at his home yesterday and that you’ve visited him there on several occasions prior to that.’

‘I went twice before,’ I said. ‘On one occasion by arrangement, and the second time, he wasn’t in.’ I tried to recall the dates, but couldn’t.

‘Oh?’

‘And when I went there yesterday, he was absent again.’ I decided to say nothing of the distant figure I had seen pacing in the garden.

‘Was there any particular reason for your visit?’

‘Not really. Other than to let him know that I’d finally decided to leave the place.’

He wrote in his notebook. ‘So on both of the previous two occasions, Alex Lister was either absent or refused you entry.’

It wasn’t what I’d told him. And again the remark suggested he knew more than he was letting on, and put me on my guard.

‘He told me when I first visited him that he has days when he simply doesn’t want company. He seemed depressed, at least unhappy.’

‘Was there any particular reason for that, do you think?’ He tapped his chin with the pen.

‘He lost his wife,’ I said. ‘I always imagined it was something from which he’d never properly recovered.’

‘Right,’ he said. ‘If you don’t mind me saying, you seem to know a lot about someone you say you hardly know—someone who might have gone out of his way to actually *avoid* you.’ He looked directly at me, waiting for my response. Again, it wasn’t what I’d told him—about Alex Lister avoiding me—and I wondered who in the village he had already spoken to.

‘Because in addition to my visits to his home, I’ve seen him out here,’ I said. ‘Walking.’ I tried to remember how many times I’d encountered Alex Lister in the dunes and on the beach.

‘That’s interesting,’ he said. ‘Any idea where he might have been going?’

‘I got the impression that he was just walking. Between the village and the sea, that’s all.’

‘I see,’ he said.

My patience with all this evasion and suggestion was at an end. ‘Has something happened to him?’ I said.

‘Not so far as we know.’ He finally closed his pad. ‘The simple fact is, he’s not been seen for a few days, that’s all. His sister called us. She lives in the Midlands. She was concerned. He hasn’t answered her calls for over a week now. I went to the address earlier. The door was locked and he wasn’t home. The woman who runs the shop said you’d been there yesterday. That’s really why I’m here. At this stage, we’re just trying to establish when he was last seen. This is all probably something and nothing—these things usually are—but we have a statutory duty to fulfil. You can imagine how worried his sister is.’

‘I didn’t even know he *had* any family,’ I said. ‘All I ever heard him mention was his lost wife.’

‘I see. It was twelve years ago. His sister says it hit him hard.’

‘I imagine it did,’ I said. ‘I mean, it did.’ *Twelve years.* I had always imagined the death of the woman to have been considerably more recent. *Recently*—it was the word he himself had used.

‘And he definitely didn’t respond when you called at his home yesterday?’ he said.

‘Ask Mrs Owen,’ I said. ‘She and another woman watched me all the time I was there.’

‘Watched you? Why would they do that?’

I shrugged. ‘She saw me knock and wait and then come away.’

‘And where did you go afterwards?’

‘I came back here. Along the paths.’ I decided then, in light of what he had just told me about Alex Lister being missing—and regardless of what any contradiction of my previous story might now imply to him—to reveal to him what I had seen on my way back to the sea.

He sensed something of my hesitation and waited.

‘I saw him,’ I said simply.

‘Sorry?’

‘Alex Lister. From the embankment. A few hundred yards beyond the end of his garden. I walked along it. I looked back and saw him—at least I assumed it was him—standing in the middle of his overgrown lawn.'

'From what distance would you say that was?'

'Four hundred yards, perhaps. You can go and check it.'

'I doubt there's any call for that,' he said. 'And you're certain it was him, Alex Lister?'

'Not a hundred per cent,' I said. 'But who else would it be?'

'It was a hot day, hazy. Perhaps it was further than four hundred yards. That's almost a quarter of a mile. It's a long way.'

'Does his sister think something might have happened to him?' I said. 'Was he expected somewhere? Has this kind of thing—'

'I don't think anything of that nature's been suggested.'

'But why would she call the police?'

The question and all it implied remained unanswered. He went back to the door and looked across the road to the sea.

'Will you get in touch?' he said. 'If you hear from him.'

'Of course.'

He came back to me and gave me a card. 'If he comes back out here, for instance. Or if you go back to the village and find him at home.'

'I daresay Mrs Owen would see him before anyone else,' I said.

'I suppose so. I've done my best to reassure his sister, but you know how these things are. At least what you've told me today should help. She's much older than her brother, bound to be concerned.'

I saw how little his empty reassurances would achieve with the woman.

'And you're here for at least another week?' he said.

'That's right. Will you let me know?' I said.

'Know?'

'When Alex Lister turns up.'

'Of course. You'll see—I'll get back to Eastleigh and someone will already have called to tell us where he is.' He went outside and stood for a moment looking up and down the beach, before walking back to his car and driving away.

Chapter Seventeen

I slept badly again, waking from a dream of Alex Lister pacing in his untended garden. Pacing, gesticulating frantically and shouting to me from that distance. I could hear nothing of what he shouted, only sense his anger and his great distress. I watched him from where I stood on the embankment, and then I turned my back on him, happy to leave him and his blighted existence as far behind me as possible.

I woke the instant he suddenly and inexplicably appeared directly in front of me, and when I could hear his shouting voice to the exclusion of all else. My mind raced with everything the constable had said and implied, and I remembered my every conversation with the missing man, and they too played over and over in my head—both in my unsettled, confused dreaming and in my uncertain, waking thoughts.

I lay awake as the sky brightened, and then as the sun again rose clear and vivid over the horizon. There had been speculation in the previous day's paper that the long, unbroken spell of weather—the warmest two months for over fifty years, the experts said—was soon to end. The late-summer pressure systems were reasserting themselves and cooler winds were about to blow.

By seven, almost as though to presage these predictions, the sun, previously sitting in a pale, clear sky, was surrounded by thin cloud. By eight, this cloud had gathered and thickened and the sun had all but disappeared within it.

Soon after this, I went outside and searched the horizon all around me—though whether in search of this imminent change in the season or in the faint hope of seeing Alex Lister wandering there, I was uncertain. I knew this latter was unlikely. Equally unlikely was the notion that the police might now be actively searching for the man. Besides, even if he had returned home after his short, unexplained absence, I was also unlikely to be informed of the fact. The man's sister might be distantly concerned, but no one else would be.

I felt the change in the weather. A wind blew the grass in the dunes all day, and sand settled in new rippled patterns across the ground around my chalet. I saw the change in the sea—a darkening of its surface now that the cloud had thickened, and an increase in the height and frequency of its breaking waves. I heard it, too, in the energy of the deepening swell and the churning of the pebbles beneath the water.

It was still warm enough for me to sit outside for most of the morning, but by early afternoon the wind had risen sufficiently to send me indoors. I understood in less than an hour of this confinement what a claustrophobic place the chalet would become once cut off from its surroundings in the coming seasons. The place then would more resemble a vessel out on the unpredictable ocean rather than a refuge on the land. I stood at my window and watched the cloud darken even further across the horizon.

No rain came, but by early evening it was clear to me that a change had taken place, that somewhere in the greater cycle of things, a balance had been tipped.

As the sun fell, the sky brightened briefly, showing clear across its landward horizon, but this lasted for only ten or twenty minutes before the darkness was complete.

Over the sea, however, a distant, much darker band had formed, and this only thickened and came closer to the shore the further the sun fell away from it. I knew the coast suffered from seasonal mists—*frets* they were called locally—and I wondered if this was one of them—a low, gentle mist that often came and went with the rising and the turning of the tide.

Because of my restless night, I fell asleep early, and woke several hours later in the darkness. It was almost ten, and because the sun was long since gone and the cloud had thickened even further, it was considerably darker than I was accustomed to.

I looked outside and saw that the bank of distant cloud or mist had come no closer to the shore. I surprised myself by being disappointed by this. The mist—if that is what it was—might have rolled towards the shore and then over the land beyond and buried me completely. I would have known then for certain that a change had come, that the true summer was over and that the early autumn was starting to assert itself. It would have been a kind of marker, a junction—something to better define the end of my time there. But instead the sky above the coast, though dark, was clear.

I felt the chill of the chalet now that it had not been heated by a day of sun, and I was surprised to discover how swiftly and completely all the residual heat had gone from the fabric of the place.

I lit my lanterns and carried in more fuel for my stove. I felt better rested now, and hungry. And unlike the previous night, I had not dreamed of Alex Lister and what he might have been trying to communicate to me in all his angry shouting.

I was about to return indoors from my wood-gathering, when I heard a distant call. I put down my load and walked beyond the flimsy lean-to. The noise had come from the direction of the chalets already lost to the dunes. I waited, searching the darkness and cupping my ear in an effort to hear more.

After several minutes of this, and hearing nothing further, I was about to go back indoors when I finally heard something else. This time it sounded like breaking wood. And soon after this, I distinctly heard several shouting voices.

I went to the end of the garden, where my view out over the abandoned buildings was unbroken, and from there I saw a light in the distance—two lights—torches perhaps, vanishing and then reappearing in the darkness. I heard the voices again. I waited, glancing back to see how much of my own light showed through the small rear window. There was a glow there, but only a dim one. Where I stood, twenty yards from the building, I would be completely invisible in the darkness.

The shouting grew louder, and the silence between individual voices was now filled with laughter. More small lights appeared, and I guessed by the flickering nature of these that they were naked flames. People were in the dunes—the village youths, most likely—lighting fires again. I wondered if there was any connection between all this nocturnal activity and the predicted ending of the summer. Perhaps it was a night of farewell celebrations by everyone who would soon be leaving the place. Or perhaps it was something that had happened before during my stay there, but which I had never previously heard.

As I watched, one of the distant lights grew much larger—a proper blaze now—and then continued growing until I realised that a building itself had been set alight. I knew how easily the desiccated woodwork and panelling would burn, how swiftly every wind-dried fitting and wall would be consumed once set alight. I knew, too, what fuel the pitch-covered roofs would add to any blaze.

Within minutes, the fire was raging in the darkness, filling the air with its glowing embers, and crackling and crashing as the chalet burned.

I left my garden and walked to the edge of the dunes. The blaze was still high. I saw the dozen or so figures moving around it, gathering up and throwing fuel on to the flames. I recognised the voice of Mary Owen. Boys shouted for attention as they dragged and threw heavier timbers on to the blaze. Each silence was filled with excited calling and screaming and laughter.

I knew before arriving at the fire which of the chalets had been targeted for the blaze. It was the most substantial of the structures still standing, the one that would burn the brightest and longest. And when it was finally consumed, reduced to ashes, then so too, perhaps, would a great deal else finally be gone from the place.

I heard the sound of shattering glass, and watched as a sudden fountain of sparks rose into the air above. I saw where the night breeze blew burning embers in a wide arc across the sand. These settled over a great distance and continued to burn. I heard the screams of girls as they ran to the seaward side of the blaze to avoid the floating embers.

All this lasted at least an hour, after which the fire subsided and the mound at its centre settled lower to the ground.

The small crowd grew quieter and then gathered together closer to the glowing ashes. I imagined they had brought drink with them, and that the party or celebration would now continue for as long as this lasted, and for as long as the dying blaze continued to warm everyone there.

Still unseen, I returned to my chalet. My skin was chilled, and even sitting close to my own small fire did little to warm me. Outside in the dunes, the shouting voices fell silent. I understood then what a charmed existence I had led in the place—one of choice and ease and warmth—but that all of this would now soon and swiftly end. The remainder of the autumn would come, and after that winter would settle like a cold sheet over everything. The spring would return, of course, and then another summer, but by then it would all be too late, and the last watching presence in the place would finally be gone from it.

The smell of smoke filled the air, and the disturbed gulls came and went in the darkness all around me, their strange and fleeting shapes illuminated briefly in the fire's dying glow. For the first time since my arrival, I knew that I had company close by, and yet it seemed to me that I was more alone than ever in that empty place, and that both the land and the sea around me were endless in their darkness.

Chapter Eighteen

By the morning, the bank of low cloud that had yesterday filled the eastern horizon had finally drifted in over the sea and across the beach and the road and now surrounded me in all directions. I could make out the sea wall ahead of me, but not the shoreline beyond it. I could see the closer half of my lost rear garden, but not its distant fence, and certainly nothing of the fields or the drains beyond.

The mist spread to the left and to the right of me. I could make out the dim shapes of the chalets closest to me, but nothing further. The road faded imperceptibly into nothingness in both directions. Above me, though I could distinguish between the darkness lower down and the brightness of the sky above, I could see nothing of the risen sun. I felt the damp chill of the mist on my face. The sand which the previous day had blown and drifted all around me was now still at my feet. Likewise, whereas yesterday I had heard the breaking waves beneath me, now there was only silence; every sound, it seemed, suppressed and then muted by this enveloping cloud.

I crossed the wall and climbed on to the sea wall. The sand immediately beneath me was in sight, but not the water. I had no way of telling how far the cloud that had flowed over me in the night now stretched inland. I saw by the smooth and compact nature of the sand that the tide in the night had been a high one.

I walked back and forth along the wall and called out. I expected an echo, but none came.

Climbing down, I followed the road towards the dunes and then to the burned-out chalet. A mound of blackened timber and grey ash lay in an almost perfect circle. Nothing remained upright; everything had burned and fallen and burned again. Here and there a spar or thin joist showed amid the wreckage, but everything else had been consumed and lost. Smoke still rose from the centre of this low mound, and in places it still glowed and flared beneath its dark crust. I pulled a pole from a nearby ruin and prodded at the remains. Sparks rose and then swiftly died.

The first strong wind would scatter the cold ashes, and afterwards everything would be lost beneath a layer of sand. By the end of the winter, there would be nothing left to see, certainly nothing of the building itself, and perhaps nothing even to mark where it had once stood. I prodded again at the mound of ash, throwing up more sparks; small, exhausted flames came briefly to life. The stories that had once attached themselves to the place might not die so swiftly or so completely as *it* had now gone, but there would no longer be any tangible focus for those tales, nowhere for them to stake their claim.

I circled the wreckage and then walked further into the dunes. Empty bottles and cans lay scattered on the slopes. I saw where the sand had been trodden and flattened by people sitting on it. Smaller mounds of ash and charred timber revealed where other fires had been lit. Further footprints created their own insubstantial paths back towards the fields and the village. I expected to come across huddled, sleeping bodies, but there was no one.

I was about to turn back and await the lifting of the mist when I saw a movement ahead of me, at the very edge of my vision, no more than twenty feet away. I waited where I stood. My immediate impression was that it was a woman, and that she was walking with great difficulty through the soft sand. I watched her, hoping I hadn't been seen, that she might continue walking and then be lost to me in the surrounding cloud. But instead she came closer to me, towards the remains of the fire, and I soon recognised Mary Owen. She was walking barefoot and carrying a solitary shoe.

She paused, looked up and saw me ahead of her. She stopped walking for a moment and then came to stand beside me at the edge of the smoking remains. She crouched down and held out her palms to feel the last of their warmth.

'That's that, then,' she said, finally acknowledging my presence.

'Were you here all night?' I asked her.

She motioned to the dunes. 'I fell asleep. Most of us did.' She held up the shoe to me. 'I lost my shoe.'

'I saw you,' I said. 'I saw what you did.'

'What we did? We burned the place down, that's all. It happens practically every year.'

'Not with this one,' I said.

She looked back to the fire. 'No, well . . . ' She took out her phone and held it up to me. 'We all took pictures.'

I went closer to her to look. 'Did you know the fog would come in?' I asked her.

'The fret?' She shrugged. 'It happens every year. It's early this year, that's all. Besides, this is nothing. At the end of the autumn, there are some mornings when you can hardly see your hand in front of your face. Have you seen it?'

'Seen what?'

'My shoe.' She pushed the phone back into her pocket.

I shook my head.

She rose and walked in a full circle around the lost chalet, after which she turned towards the sea, her eyes back on the ground, searching.

'Someone said you were leaving,' she said over her shoulder to me.

'Soon.'

'Might as well,' she said. 'You had the best of a good year. You wouldn't want what's coming next.'

She wandered further ahead of me until we both arrived at the beach, where she finally abandoned her searching.

The breaking tide was still invisible, but I sensed that the mist was now slowly starting to thin; I could see more of the beach than when I had first come out.

'Is it lifting?' I asked her.

'Probably. The sun gets up and starts to break it down.' She dropped her shoe and carried on walking towards the invisible water.

'What will you do?' I asked her. 'Once the others leave?'

She considered the question before answering me. 'I'll do what everybody does,' she said, anger rising briefly in her voice.

The sea appeared ahead of us, and she walked into it until it rose to her shins. I knew how cold it must have been beyond the reach of the sun.

I followed her towards the water's edge and waited there. She hummed to herself for a moment and then fell silent. I struggled for something further to say to her, and just as I was about to invite her back to the chalet, she called out to me and started wading through the water, splashing as she went.

I called to ask her what she was doing, what she'd seen.

'There's something there,' she said, pointing ahead of her.

I followed her hand and saw a shape at the water's edge further up the beach, something half-submerged in the water and half-concealed by the mist.

Approaching closer to this, she stopped and then clasped both her arms across her chest.

'What is it?' I called to her.

'You'll have to—' She stopped abruptly, and then turned and splashed her way back to the shore.

I waited for her at the water's edge, and when she reached me she grabbed my arm.

'What is it?' I asked her again.

She looked at me hard for a few seconds, and then said, simply, 'A body.'

'Are you sure?'

She continued to hold on to me. I looked over her shoulder to where the shape in the water moved slowly in the swell.

My first thought was that it was one of her friends from the previous night, drunk and careless, who had perhaps fallen asleep too close to the approaching tide. But before I could say anything, she said, 'It's Alex Lister.'

I looked back to the gently bobbing shape.

'Are you sure? I mean—'

'It's him,' she said. She pulled herself away from me, and released from her grip I went closer to the body.

I waded into cold water until Alex Lister's floating corpse touched my legs. He was face-down and I turned him so that he was revealed to me and so that there could be no mistake.

A first glimmer of sunlight illuminated us as a small patch of clear sky finally appeared above us. I reached down and held his shoulder, pulling him back towards the beach, where he finally lay and became impossible to move any further.

'He went missing,' I said, knowing how ridiculous this sounded, and already piecing together the scant, dark details of the man's final few unhappy days.

But she wasn't listening to me; instead she was on her phone, telling someone what we'd found.

When she stopped talking, she turned to me and said we'd been told to stay where we were.

And so we stood together and we waited like that, with Alex Lister's body only a few feet from us, his face already half-buried in the damp sand as the sea continued its retreat. We waited as the mist lifted and as the coming day slowly brightened around us, neither of us speaking, neither of us moving, until an hour later, when two police cars and an ambulance, all three with their lights flashing, finally appeared and made their way silently towards us—to where the dark and reliable surface of the road ended and where the pale, rippled patterns of the drifting sand began.

Robert Edric was born in 1956. His novels include *Winter Garden* (James Tait Black Prize winner 1986), *A New Ice Age* (runner-up for the Guardian Fiction Prize 1986), *The Book of the Heathen* (winner of the WH Smith Literary Award 2000), *Peacetime* (longlisted for the Booker Prize 2002), *Gathering the Water* (longlisted for the Booker Prize 2006), and three linked novels about crime: *Cradle Song*, *Siren Song* and *Swan Song*. He is one of the most critically admired novelists of his generation. His novel, *In Zodiac Light*, based on the life of the WWI composer and poet Ivor Gurney was shortlisted for the 2010 International IMPAC Dublin Literary Award. *The London Satyr* was selected as one of the 2011 'Fiction Uncovered' titles.